W9-APE-346

Cinderella
CLEANERS
Swan Fake

Read all the Cinderella Cleaners books!

Change of a Dress

Prep Cool

Rock & Role

Mask Appeal

Scheme Spirit

Swan Fake

MAYA GOLD

SCHOLASTIC INC.
New York Toronto London Auckland
Sydney Mexico City New Delhi Hong Kong

ISBN 978-0-545-22769-8

12 11 10 9 8 7 6 5 4 3 2 1 11 12 13 14 15 16/0

Printed in the U.S.A. 40
First edition, January 2011

Book design by Yaffa Jaskoll

For Actors & Writers
(and singers and dancers)

Chapter One

For my stepmother, Fay, the day after Thanksgiving is all about Black Friday shopping bargains. But I think the best deal around is not having to set my alarm clock.

It isn't that I don't like school, but the end of November is totally crazed. Teachers are loading on term papers and preparing us for everyone's favorite (not!): midterm exams. By the time we get to winter vacation, just three weeks away, the whole eighth grade will collapse in a heap. I can't imagine how I could possibly do one more thing.

But today I don't have to! If I knew how to purr, I would. Instead, I take a luxurious stretch, looking lazily out the window of my attic bedroom. The trees are all bare except for a few clinging leaves, and I can see the roof of Dad's car in the driveway below, so he's still at home.

I pull on my red bathrobe and head downstairs, being careful to tiptoe past my twin stepsisters' bedroom. Ashley and Brynna love to sleep late, and my fingers are crossed that they'll stay in their bunk beds all morning so I have some privacy.

Dad's at the kitchen counter, pouring the last inch of coffee into a Sam's Diner travel mug. He's dressed for work — Black Friday isn't a holiday when you own a dry-cleaning business like Cinderella Cleaners.

"Up so early, Diana?" he says, faking shock. His raised eyebrows and wide eyes remind me so much of my grandpapa that I can't help smiling. Papa and Nonni just flew up from Florida for a surprise Thanksgiving visit. They took off early this morning — Papa insisted on driving their rental car straight to Newark Airport with "no hammy good-bye scenes." I miss them already.

"Fay should be done shopping by lunchtime," Dad says. "But if you get hungry, there are plenty of leftovers."

This is the understatement of the century. My Italian grandmother made three trays of lasagna as well as the usual turkey and stuffing, candied yams, pumpkin pie, and the rest.

"Thanks, Dad," I tell him. "I don't think we'll starve."

"Have fun with the girls," he says, kissing the top of my head. "They really look up to you."

Right, I think. *Only because I'm half a foot taller.* But I don't want to rain on Dad's parade, so I just smile as he heads out the door.

I have several delicious hours before Fay gets back home. Finally, a chance to practice my song for the Drama Club's upcoming musical, *The Snow Queen*, without anyone bugging me.

I've been acting and singing since I was in preschool, and there's nothing that makes me feel better. I wasn't in the fall play, *Our Town*, because I had to work after school at the cleaners, so I'm determined to shine in this one. Our drama advisor, Ms. Wyant, gave me a very cool role: I'm the Enchantress who casts a magic spell over the royal kingdom, turning spring into winter. It's also a very small role, because I can only go to the last five rehearsals, what we call tech week.

I down a quick glass of orange juice and head back upstairs, stopping to look in my bedroom mirror. There

I am, with my boring brown hair, brown eyes and eyebrows, a tallish but otherwise perfectly ordinary-looking thirteen-year-old girl. I used to envy my three closest friends, who all have more striking coloring: Jess Munson is a flaming redhead, Amelia Williams is a natural blonde with surprising brown eyes, and Sara Parvati is Indian, with gorgeous dark eyes and a waterfall of black hair.

But I've learned there are advantages to plain brown and brown. I can make myself look like a lot of different people, and that's come in handy again and again, not just onstage, but in real life, too. My after-school job at Cinderella Cleaners has offered me plenty of chances to dress up in customers' garments — something I've *promised* my dad I will not do again — and I've managed to pass for somebody else every time.

I'm still wrapped in my red plush bathrobe, which makes me feel glamorous, as if I were lounging backstage in a Broadway dressing room instead of in a suburban house in Weehawken, New Jersey, the plain brown hair of places to be from. But I love my room. One side of the ceiling is slanted, which makes it feel like a secret clubhouse. I've wallpapered that section with *Playbills* from every Broadway show I've ever seen, and on the opposite wall I've hung all of my jewelry, scarves, and accessories. My bedspread is the same turquoise blue as the ocean across from my grandparents' condo.

I start out by doing the vocal warm-ups Ms. Wyant taught us. Some are tongue twisters (say very fast, *"The tip of the tongue, the teeth, and the lips"*), and some are sounds like *"Maaa, may, meee, mo, moooo."* But my favorites are nonsense songs, like *"Fish and chips and vinegar, fish and chips and vinegar, pepper, pepper, pepper, pop!"*

They're a little like cheerleading chants, I realize. Not too long ago, when I thought all cheerleaders were snobs with attitude, this would have embarrassed me big-time. But now that I've met some very nice varsity cheerleaders, I don't feel the same way about it. I'm almost a little bit proud.

That is, until I remember our middle school's cheerleading captain, Kayleigh Carell, who's playing the Snow Queen and thinks that makes her queen of the rest of the universe. She really *is* a cheerleader snob with attitude. You can't assume that clichés are true, but Kayleigh is living proof that sometimes they're right on the money.

I shudder, trying to put the Drama Club's so-called star out of my mind as I reach into my book bag. Miss Bowman, the music teacher, burned a rehearsal CD of the piano accompaniment to my song, so I can work on it at home. I put in the CD and listen to Miss Bowman playing the opening chords. How does an enchantress *move*, I wonder? Does she have a wand or a tall magic staff that she leans on? Ms. Wyant and I haven't talked about costuming yet, and I never feel like I'm inside a character's skin till I know what she wears.

In my mind's eye, I picture a long cloak or cape, something silvery white and wintry. Will the fabric be silken and shimmery, or stiff and high-collared with heavy embroidery? The first one would move like a snake in the water, all slinky and cool. The second would be more regal.

But I have to stop thinking about clothes and start singing. In spite of my warm-ups, the first notes sound strained. It's been a long time since I sang anything tougher than "Happy Birthday." It's not till I get to the chorus, with its dramatic long notes of "*snow, falling snooooow*" that my voice opens up.

And the next thing I hear is "Shut UP!" from below.

Oops. Woke the twins.

So much for rehearsing in private. I sigh and turn off the CD, calling out "Sorry!" as I head downstairs.

Ashley and Brynna are outside their bedroom, dressed in matching pajamas. They aren't identical, but their looks are so close that sometimes it's quicker to read their body language than it is to squint and see which one is blonder, who's got more freckles, and whose hair is an inch or two shorter.

Ashley, born seventeen minutes before her twin, is always the boss. She tends to position herself a step or two farther forward, usually frowning, with Brynna, a little more cringing and whiny, behind.

"Good morning," I say.

Ashley says, "You woke me up," in accusing tones, while Brynna rubs her eyes, droning, "I was asleeeep."

My dad is a sensible guy, but if these girls look up to me, I'm a baboon. They wish I'd get out of their lives is more like it, and often the feeling is mutual.

I always used to wish I had a sister. That was before I got two. And a stepmother.

By the time Fay returns from her shopping spree, laden with bags and complaining nonstop, it's hard to remember why I was so happy about staying home.

But Monday comes soon enough. I drag through my morning classes on autopilot, filling the margins of my notebook with costume sketches for the Enchantress. At long last it's time for lunch.

As I enter the cafeteria, I look around for my friend — well, maybe a little bit more than a friend — Will Carson, but he's nowhere in sight. That flutter of anticipation followed by disappointment reminds me that Will *is* something more than a friend, even if neither of us has a clue what to call it.

When I arrive at my usual lunch table, Jess and Sara are there. Jess is packing a PB&J, pretzels, and one of the foil-covered Suncup juices her mother always brings home from the hospital where she works. Sara's family owns the best Indian restaurant in northern New Jersey, and her lunches are always mouthwatering. But she gets sick of the same menu leftovers day after day, so sometimes I can swap my tuna sandwich for gourmet Indian takeout. No luck today, though: My sandwich is filled with the last of our Thanksgiving feast, and everyone's burned out on turkey and cranberry sauce by now. Sara takes one look and decides to hang on to her homemade *pakoras* and coconut shrimp. Amelia, as always, is standing in line for the hot lunch. I can see her blond ponytail and favorite Spain World Cup jersey as she disappears into the hidden lair of the lunch ladies.

Ever since *Snow Queen* rehearsals began, a couple of Drama Club boys have been joining our foursome: Riley, a lanky African-American boy with the best singing voice in the cast, and Ethan, a funny but slightly conceited boy I've known since preschool. They're playing father and son, and according to Jess, who fills me in nightly on all the backstage drama I'm missing, they both have crushes on a petite seventh grader named Marisol who's playing Ethan's love interest. Apparently Marisol doesn't think much of Prince Ethan offstage, but she's all swoony-eyed over King Riley. Who, being a typically clueless thirteen-year-old boy, doesn't know what to say to her and just clams up.

This makes perfect sense to me, because ever since I realized Will and I both like each other, we've turned into mutes whenever we meet. In fact, there he is now, coming out from the lunch line!

Just the sight of Will shaking his too-long bangs out of his eyes while he juggles his backpack and lunch tray makes me blush all the way to the tips of my ears. I hope he'll sit next to me, though I'd be completely embarrassed to ask him out loud.

Jess, Ethan, and Riley are loudly rehashing some story about a sixth grader who flubbed several lines yesterday, causing Kayleigh, the Snow Queen, to be late for her entrance.

"That kid is my *hero*," says Ethan, who went out with Kayleigh for a short time and now grabs any chance he can get to make fun of Her Highness. "You think I could hire him to do that on opening night?"

"Did you see the look on her face?" says Jess, hooting with laughter.

"Wish I could've snapped a pic with my phone and posted it on Facebook," Riley says. "Can you imagine?"

Ethan slaps him five and they all crack up.

Will's reached our table. He glances at the three laughing actors and points at the seat between Sara and me. "Is this saved for Amelia?"

We both shake our heads. I try not to grin, but I'm thinking *Hooray!* as Will sits down. He's wearing a T-shirt that I've never seen. Every day he wears shirts with logos of his favorite bands (a *very* long list, since his dad's in the music business, and Will and his brother play bass and guitar), but today's is plain white, with a graphic of an eye with a crown.

"What does that mean?" I ask, and he looks confused. I point to his T-shirt.

Will looks down at his chest, as if he's got no idea what he pulled out of his dresser this morning — which, knowing Will Carson, he probably doesn't.

"Oh," he mumbles. "Cat Empire. Great band from Australia."

I can't help smiling. Of *course* it's a band!

"Cool," I say, nodding. And then I run clean out of things to say to him. We sit side by side, and the silence between us just stretches.

Luckily, Sara jumps into it. "What's the hot lunch?" she asks, looking down at Will's plate. "Eggplant parm?"

Will shrugs. "Something parm. I forgot to ask." He scoops up a forkful and chews, looking puzzled. "Not sure. Might be chicken?"

Amelia arrives at our table with her lunch tray. "Okay, it's official," she says, pulling a chair from a neighboring table to sit on the far side of Sara. "The Weehawken Middle School cafeteria just hit an all-time low. Door number one: chicken poppers. Door number two, for all you vegetarians: bread parmesan."

Will coughs a little. "*Bread* parmesan?"

Amelia looks at his plate. "Will, you *got* it?"

"I thought it was chicken," Will says.

"Nope," says Amelia, lifting something that looks like a fried malted milk ball. "*This* is supposed to be chicken."

"Bread parmesan, wow," Sara says, eyeing Will's sauce-covered lunch. "Want to split a samosa?"

"Or turkey?" I ask. "It's the last gasp of Thanksgiving dinner."

Will shakes his head, saying, "I'm good. But thanks."

Jess, Ethan, and Riley are still trading can-you-top-this-one rehearsal stories, and I have to admit that I'm feeling a little left out. I'm in this play, too, after all.

As if reading my thoughts, Will leans over and asks, "Have you gotten to practice your solo with Miss Bowman yet?"

"Tomorrow," I tell him, my heart feeling instantly lighter.

"Cool," says Will.

"I don't know why I'm so nervous about it. My song is like three minutes long."

" 'Cause you care," says Will. "I'm the same way when I have a solo, even if it's just a couple of notes. You don't want to be the one messing things up."

"Exactly," I say, and we look at each other. Will's much too shy to act or sing lead — he's on the sound crew for *The Snow Queen*. Even the instruments he plays (bass guitar and euphonium) are supporting actors, not stars. But he totally gets it.

"What are you guys talking about?" Amelia asks. Neither she nor Sara gets the whole theatre thing. They live and breathe soccer. Sara also studies Indian dance, but Amelia's all sports, all the time. Her favorite subject is gym. Which is kind of ironic, since her big sister Zoe's a super-obsessed ballerina, and so was Amelia's mother. They even persuaded Amelia to dance a small part in a local dance company's performance of *The Nutcracker*, and she's been griping about it for weeks.

"Just *Snow Queen* stuff," I reply. "My solo."

Instead of responding, Amelia gives me a funny look.

"Ask her," says Sara, nudging Amelia's arm.

"Ask me what?" I say, trying not to drip cranberry sauce on my napkin.

Amelia sets down her fork. "It's a really big favor."

She's got my attention. I swallow. "What is it?"

Amelia sighs. "You know how I got roped into doing this *Nutcracker* thing?"

Speak of the devil. I nod, waiting for more.

"Well, the only reason I did it was so Mom would let me go to this incredible soccer intensive with Sara over winter break."

"I did it last year," Sara says. "It was sick."

Amelia goes on. "We just found out the soccer tryouts are a week from Saturday, from one to two-thirty." I nod again. Where is she heading with this? "That's the same afternoon as *The Nutcracker*'s matinee performance. Which starts at two."

"Oh, you're kidding," I say sympathetically. "That totally bites." Will nods.

"Could you do it for me?" says Amelia.

For a moment I don't even know what she's asking. Do what? Then it dawns on me. My stomach drops in shock. "You want me to *dance ballet*?"

This is totally out of the question. I went to ballet school for maybe a year, when I was about six years old. After the first recital (the one where I tripped), I switched over to tap dance and never looked back.

Besides, Amelia just said *The Nutcracker* is a week from Saturday. So there's *really* no way. "That's the opening night of *The Snow Queen*!" I tell her.

"I know, but that starts at seven o'clock," Amelia replies quickly. "This is at two. You'd have plenty of time in between, and you just finished saying you've only got one song. Plus there's nobody else I can ask. I'm desperate."

This is a tough one. Amelia stuck her neck out to help me sneak into a recent Halloween ball, and I really owe her a favor. But dancing *ballet*? When I have an opening night just a few hours later?

"I don't know, Amelia," I tell her. "I'd love to help out, but ballet isn't something you can fake."

"Of course it is," Amelia laughs. "When I was little, I used to mess up the name of the ballet *Swan Lake* and call it *Swan Fake*. My mom would go, '*Lake*. It's Swan *Lake*!' But I was faking it then, and I'm faking it now, trust me."

I'm feeling overwhelmed. I need some details. "What are you playing, again?" I ask. "Some kind of toy?"

Amelia nods. "A mechanical doll. I have a small role in the opening scene, where they take me out of a gift box and wind me up. I dance a few steps and slow down to a stop." She makes a robot movement, then freezes, head cocked to one side. "And I'll be back in plenty of time for Act Two, when I have to actually dance."

That does sound like something I could swan-fake, if

it wasn't for *The Snow Queen* being right after. I try a new tack. "But I don't look anything like you."

"Diana, I'm playing a *doll*. My face will be painted, I'm wearing a wig, and I move like a windup toy. No one would know you're not me."

"Not even your mom?" I ask.

Amelia just snorts. "She won't pay any attention to *me* — Zoe is dancing the lead."

I'm running out of excuses. "But doesn't your mom know these soccer tryouts are on the same day?"

"Oh, yes," says Sara.

"We've been fighting about it all weekend," Amelia explains. "No way would I have agreed to this *Nutcracker* thing if I'd known it meant missing the soccer trials, but now that I'm in it, Mom tells me I've 'made a commitment' " — Amelia makes air quotes with her fingers — "and 'the show must go on.' "

"She's right," I say. "Imagine if you skipped out on a soccer game. It would stink for the rest of the team."

Will nods again. He's been listening to this whole exchange, and I know he's imagining what it would do to a band if the bass player didn't show up for a gig.

Amelia agrees. "No, I get it, I know. I just want to do *both.* And I can. Just not before two o'clock. Actually, I have to be in full costume and makeup by one-thirty."

Full costume and makeup? That does sound like fun. . . .

I hesitate, looking at Will for support. I do like the idea of saving the day for Amelia. That's what friends do for each other, right? They help even when it's not easy. But not when it's downright impossible. Among other issues — like how much trouble we'd both be in if we got caught — there's a chance Dad will need me to work for a few hours that Saturday. The preholiday season is a dry cleaner's busiest time of year.

"Well?" says Amelia. "Can you be me?"

"Please?" Sara adds.

They're both looking at me with pleading eyes. I take a deep breath. "Can I let you know after work?" I ask.

"Um, sure," says Amelia. "As long as the answer is yes."

"But no pressure," says Will with a smile.

Yeah, right!

Chapter Two

The bus ride from school to Cinderella Cleaners always helps me clear my head. On the way down the hill, there's a fabulous view of the Manhattan skyline, with the Empire State Building glinting in late-afternoon winter sun. As I gaze at the glamorous city, I try to imagine what it would be like to pass myself off as Amelia and dance in *The Nutcracker*. One half of my brain fills with a gauzy fantasy in which I'm dancing with graceful perfection; the other half tells me, *Get real. You'll fall flat on your face.*

Probably true. Besides, I'm already so busy! I start making a mental list of all the things I've got on my plate. There's rehearsing my Enchantress solo . . . tech week for *The Snow Queen* . . . my job at the cleaners . . .

midterms . . . a paper for English . . . Christmas shopping for family and friends . . .

And on top of that, I'm supposed to learn a *ballet*? When, in my *sleep*?

I don't know how I could do this. But how can I say no to Amelia? There's nothing that feels worse than letting down one of your friends when they're counting on you.

Well, if Dad tells me I have to work that Saturday afternoon, the choice will be out of my hands. I guess I'll just leave it to destiny.

That makes me feel a little less stressed. I open my notebook and look at the sketches I doodled for my Enchantress costume. The drawings aren't great, and the icicle headdress I drew looks like the crown on the Statue of Liberty. I wonder if I could get Nelson Martinez to design my costume. Nelson is Cinderella Cleaners' head tailor and resident genius, who can design and sew *anything*. But he's been on overdrive lately, working part-time at the cleaners and part-time with the costume designer of superstar Tasha Kane's next music video — which, believe it or not, I'll be in! Long story, but I was in the right outfit at the right time and wound up getting cast as an extra and rocking a hot pink guitar! I can't wait to see it all finished.

Just thinking of that puts a smile on my face. So does thinking of Nelson. No matter how busy he gets, Nelson always has time for me and Catalina James, my closest friend at work. And though I live in fear of our demanding supervisor, Joy MacInerny (aka Joyless), and her new trainee, Lara Nekrasova (the only coworker I don't like), Nelson won't let them push him around. He's never mean, but he's not impressed by anyone's power trip.

The bus pulls up to my stop, right in front of Sam's Diner, a vintage classic that's been next to Cinderella Cleaners forever. As I head toward the cleaners' employee entrance, I spot two older teens walking out of the diner. The girl is petite and straight-backed, with dark hair pulled up in a high, tight bun. Even in Ugg boots, her feet have the distinctive turn-out of a ballerina. She's carrying two take-out coffees.

Right behind her is a broad-shouldered African-American boy with fade-shaved hair and one shiny gold earring, carrying an armload of stiff cardboard posters. He looks oddly familiar, but I can't imagine where I might have seen him, and he doesn't seem to recognize me. I'm totally stumped. But as he and the Ugg ballerina get into a van, I notice a waitress in the diner taping a poster inside the door. It's for the Fleet Feet Dancers' production of *The Nutcracker*.

That's the same one Amelia is in!

And I suddenly realize where I've seen Earring Boy before. He was one of many costumed volunteers from Fleet Feet at last month's Halloween ball — he was wearing a Turkish costume with a turban, so I didn't spot his fade. The girl must be a ballet student, too — she was probably one of the dancers that night — and they're driving around putting up posters in neighborhood businesses.

Feeling proud of myself for connecting the dots, I go in the employee entrance, taking my pastel green smock from the rack and leaving my backpack and coat in the locker room. I walk through the noisy back workroom saying hi to the people I work with — white-haired Mr. Chen, steam-pressing a shirt; his wife, Rose, dabbing some kind of chemical onto a stained cashmere sweater; Chris, the maintenance man, singing along with Usher on the radio as he replaces a part on a broken machine — on the way to the customer section in front.

As I push through the double doors, I take a deep breath to prepare for my first close encounter with Joyless and Lara. But neither of them even sees me come in. Joyless is busily gathering a huge mound of colorful garments from the counter. When she picks up a maroon Turkish turban, I realize with a thrill that they must be Fleet Feet's *Nutcracker* costumes! The two ballet students must have just dropped them off!

Now *that* is what I call a sign! It must be destiny telling me I should say yes to Amelia — that is, if I can.

I look over at Dad, who's taping a *Nutcracker* poster onto the big plate-glass window. Lara is standing next to him. "This vill be important new client, I am thinking," she says in her melodious Russian accent. "They vill do many shows, and perhaps they tell other performers Cinderella Clinners vill take extra care."

"Absolutely," says Dad. "The more special orders, the merrier. Thanks so much for steering them here."

"It vas nothink," says Lara, dipping her head with false modesty. *You need some acting lessons*, I think. Overdoing it much?

Just then Dad sees me and flashes his usual welcoming smile. "Isn't this fun, Diana? Lara's brought us a terrific new client. Look at all these ballet costumes!"

"They're great," I say, eyeing the pile. I wonder, which one is Amelia's? Then I hear a voice that always makes me happy.

"Did somebody say ballet costumes?" It's Nelson, coming out of the Tailoring section to see what the fuss is about. "Please tell me they're not all stinky tights." The first thing that catches his eye is the turban Joyless just put down. "Oh, that is outrageous," he says, putting it on his head. It's a strange combination with his hipster glasses and popped-collar shirt, but if anybody can pull off an out-of-the-box look, it's Nelson.

"I love it!" I tell him. Joyless is frowning. There aren't any customers in line, but she hates it when anyone acts at all playful with garments.

As usual, Nelson couldn't care less what she thinks. He's throwing a green velvet opera cloak over one shoulder, and I recognize it as the same one Fleet Feet's pompous founder, Mikhail Zaloom, wore when he made a *very* long-winded speech at the masquerade ball. "This is beautifully tailored," Nelson says. "It's much lighter than it looks. In fact, I feel like dancing."

He swoops back through the propped-open door to the Tailoring section. I hear shrieks of laughter from the two elderly seamstresses, Sadie and Loretta, and Sadie saying, "Oh, did you startle me!"

"You look like the Wizard of Oz," says Loretta. "You know, when he's reading the crystal ball, in the black-and-white part?"

Lips pursed, Miss MacInerny moves to the door of the Tailoring section, removing the doorstop. "Too much chit-chat," she mutters, and it occurs to me that she'd be well cast as Almira Gulch, the woman who tries to take Toto away on her bicycle.

The phone rings inside Dad's office, and he goes to answer it. I'll have to talk to him later. Lara flips up the hinged section of counter so she can help MacInerny tag the big ballet order. I take a step backward to let Lara pass, and she shoots me a look. "Cart is ready," she says in a tone that implies I've been standing around like a useless lump and should get to work, pronto.

I'm not going to give her the satisfaction of acting insulted, so I just smile and say thanks, as if she'd been completely polite. The cart is piled high with nonballet garments, including a hideous sequined sweater that's sure to make Cat hoot with laughter.

Just then, I see Joyless pick up an adorable harlequin dress. Could that be Amelia's doll costume? MacInerny flips it over, and sure enough, there's an oversize windup key at the back of the waistband. She squints at the note card pinned to the dress and says, "This one needs alterations."

Before she can blink, I've taken it out of her hand. "I'll bring it to Tailoring," I tell her, swinging the door shut behind me before she can protest.

The Tailoring section is its own little world, nestled snugly behind a glass door. Instead of the loud clunking of cleaning machines, the sound track here is the jittery clatter of sewing machines, plus the hip-hop and salsa Nelson prefers, played softly enough not to bother

Sadie and Loretta. There are wall racks of thread in a rainbow of colors, a cutting table, and a small try-on booth with a three-way mirror, flanked by two adjustable dressmaker forms, male and female. Nelson's draped the opera cloak over one of these, but he's still wearing the turban. It does make him look like some kind of magician.

"What have you got there, Diana?" he asks me, taking the harlequin dress from my hands. I get a good look at it for the first time as Nelson reads the note card. The fabric is pieced in satiny diamonds of pink, green, and yellow, with a fitted bodice and a short, flouncy skirt. I would so love to wear it!

"What does that say?" I ask, gesturing toward the note.

"'Bodice needs to be altered,'" says Nelson. "'The girl who'll be playing the part has a much broader back, and the sleeves are too tight.'"

"She's got really strong arms," I agree.

Nelson looks at me. "You *know* this ballet dancer?"

"It's my friend Amelia," I tell him. "And she's not a dancer at all. She's the star of our soccer team."

"Silly me," Nelson says. "And Mikhail Baryshnikov's in the World Cup?"

"Her mother and sister are both ballerinas. They're making her dance in this show," I explain. I can't stop staring at that adorable doll costume.

Nelson must notice, because the next thing out of his mouth is, "I think I'm going to need a live model for this alteration. Could you —?"

"You bet!" I tell him. Nelson hands me the dress and I take it into the dressing room, pulling the striped curtain closed as I take off my smock and school clothes. The satiny fabric feels smooth on my skin. I hold my breath, pulling up the side zipper. The bodice fits me like a glove, and I love how the skirt poufs out over its petticoat.

Now I *really* want to say yes to Amelia! I hope Dad will give me next Saturday afternoon off.

But wait. . . . Would that mean I was breaking my promise to stop borrowing customers' clothing *again*? This had nothing to do with my job when Amelia asked me, but here I am in the Tailoring section of Cinderella Cleaners, wearing her costume.

I try to be good, really truly. So why do I always wind up breaking rules?

Nelson's voice comes through the curtain. "Need help with the zipper?"

"I've got it," I answer. I open the curtain and step back out into the room.

Sadie and Loretta stop sewing at once. "What a vision!" Sadie says, clutching a hand to her chest. "Too sweet."

"You're a sight for sore eyes," Loretta agrees. "Eat you up with a spoon."

Is there something about getting older that makes people talk in clichés?

"I remember when you were this high," says Sadie, holding one hand to her waist. "Your grandfather's princess."

I rest my case.

"Thank you," I say to Sadie and Loretta, who are the nicest ladies on the planet, no matter how they talk. They beam and return to their sewing.

Nelson is looking me over. "It fits as if it were made for you," he says. "Too bad *you're* not wearing this."

I hesitate for a split second. It's just too delicious, and I know I can trust Nelson with any secret. "Well . . . I kind of might be," I say, dropping my voice.

Nelson barely blinks. "Of course you are," he says with a shrug. "Cheerleader, masquerade ball VIP, rock star, prep schooler — is there anything you *haven't* worn?"

"Says the man in the turban," I tease him.

"Lift up your arms," Nelson says. "Let me take some measurements." He picks up his measuring tape and tailor's chalk, making a few marks. It tickles a little, but I try to stand very still. "This really fits you like a charm," he says.

"But if you alter it to fit Amelia . . ."

Nelson smiles wickedly. "That's what elastic is for, *chica*." He moves the measuring tape to a different angle. He's taught me enough about tailoring that I can guess he's planning to open the darts and insert something stretchy so it'll fit both Amelia and me. Nelson really *is* a magician.

"How's *The Snow Queen* coming?" he asks, slipping a straight pin between his lips like a dangling toothpick. "Have you learned your solo?"

"In theory. But I haven't really gotten to work on my character yet."

"What is she wearing?" asks Nelson.

"I don't actually know, and it's *soon*," I tell him. "I hope it'll be something amazing."

Nelson nods. "You want me to design it?"

I've often thought Nelson was a bit of a mind reader, but this is ridiculous. "Yes!" I gasp. "That would totally rock!"

Nelson smiles, patting the shoulder of Amelia's costume. "Done. Watch those pins as you're taking it off."

I practically levitate into the workroom, pushing the cartload of garments. Cat is already at work sliding cardboard strips into shirt collars, her shiny black hair pulled back in a ponytail.

"Where have you been?" she demands, and then spots the sequined sweater on top of the cart. She lifts it up, holding it out at arm's length. "Oh, this is beyond tacky. What do you think? Vegas Night in Secaucus?"

"Wait till you see the *next* cartload," I tell her. "They're still getting tagged. It's a huge special order."

"More Santa suits?" Cat asks hopefully.

"Even better," I tell her.

"Speaking of Santa," Cat says, expertly slipping a shirt into its bag. "Have you drawn your Secret Santa card out of the stocking yet?"

I don't know what she's talking about. "What stocking?"

"The one on your dad's office door, duh," says Cat. I must still look confused, because she goes on, "I always forget that you're new here. We do this every year at the holiday party. Your dad puts a card with every employee's name into a stocking, and each of us draws one person that we buy a gift for. That way everybody gets *something*."

"I hope I get your name," I tell her.

"That would be awesome. But you can't tell me if you do. You have to find something for under ten dollars and wrap it up with the same card, so it stays a secret. Then we all try to guess who it was."

It sounds really fun. "Did you draw a card yet?" I ask.

"Not telling," Cat says with a funny little smirk that makes me wonder if she drew *my* name. I hope so!

As soon as I finish unloading the cart onto the sorting table, I roll it back out for a refill. Through the window I can see Chris on a ladder, hanging up tinsel garlands and Christmas lights. There's already an electric menorah placed inside the window, next to a Kwanzaa kinara painted in red, black, and green.

By now, Joyless and Lara have finished tagging the rest of the *Nutcracker* costumes, and two cartloads are waiting for me. I pass Lara the empty cart, getting a disdainful sneer in return. "You are slower than turtle," she mutters, keeping her voice low so the customers standing in line won't hear her being rude. As if that wasn't obnoxious enough, as she turns back to the cash register, she flashes the next man in line a big insincere smile. When Papa was visiting, he chastised Lara for not being friendly enough to her customers, and she's not taking any chances.

I wish she'd get fired. That's what *I* want from my Secret Santa.

Though I'd settle for next Saturday afternoon off.

The door to Dad's office is open, so I knock on the door frame and enter.

"Hi, honey," he smiles. "Going to pick out your Santa card?"

I nod, and he points to the big stocking hung up on the back of the door. "Don't tell anyone who you get," he says. "Not even me."

"What if I get you?" I ask, and Dad shrugs.

"Then you'll surprise me. You usually don't have much trouble with that."

Very true. But before I reach into the stocking, I ask in a casual, just-crossed-my-mind voice, "How many more Saturdays am I supposed to work?"

Dad looks at the calendar next to his desk. "You'll be done this weekend."

Score! "Not the one after?"

Dad raises his eyebrows. "You mean the day of your opening night?"

I nod, holding my breath.

"Of course not," says Dad. "You asked me for five workdays off and we traded five Saturdays. Last weekend's was four, and this week makes five. The Saturday of *The Snow Queen*, you can lie in bed all day long eating bonbons."

Or put on Amelia's costume and dance a Swan Fake. I smile. "I'll pass on the bonbons. I'll be much too nervous. But thanks."

I turn to go, almost forgetting that I'm supposed to be here for my Secret Santa card. Luckily, the striped stocking catches my eye. As I dip my hand inside, fingering the small thicket of cards, I think, *Please let it be Nelson or Cat!* But that sounds a bit greedy, so I try rephrasing my wish: *Anybody but Lara.*

I take a deep breath and pull out a red card, about two inches square, with a picture of a wrapped present. I look over my shoulder to make sure that no one's behind me, and open it up. Inside, in simple block letters, the card says: LI CHEN.

Lichen? I think, remembering the word from a recent biology unit. Lichen are symbiotic (midterm review word!) fungus and algae plants that grow on rocks. Is this some kind of trick?

Then I realize there's a space in between the *i* and the *C*. Li Chen. That must be Mr. Chen, the white-haired man who runs the steam presser. His wife, Rose, is the stain removal specialist, and she always greets me by name, but Mr. Chen barely looks up from his iron. I've always assumed he must not speak much English, but it's also possible that he's just quiet.

What am I going to give him? I don't know the first thing about Mr. Chen, except that he's great at his job. In all these months working here, I never even found out that his first name was Li.

Okay, well, Secret Santa has got a mission. Find out what Mr. Li Chen likes.

I roll the first load of ballet costumes into the back room, and as I expected, Cat goes nuts for them. She's never studied ballet, but one Christmas when she was little, her parents dressed her and her sisters and brothers in their Sunday best and took them across the river to see the New York City Ballet production of *The Nutcracker*. My parents did the same thing for me — once for *The Nutcracker*, once for *Swan Lake* — and even all these years later, Cat and I can remember enough of *The Nutcracker* plot to recognize some of the costumes.

"These must be the toy soldiers," she says, picking up some red jackets. "And those are the mice."

I remember the Mouse King in that production had more than one head, and he was carried in on the shoulders of a whole group of mice, making gestures with long-fingered hands. I must have been pretty little, because he showed up in my nightmares for months.

Several mouse costumes are stained at the neck, probably from greasepaint makeup, and I take them back to Rose Chen, being careful to study her husband.

As usual, he's bending over his pressing machine, cuffing a pair of pants. There are several more pairs of trousers awaiting his expert sharp crease, along with a pleated skirt. I wonder how he learned this specialty, and how long he's been doing it. I notice that he's wearing flat black cotton slippers, the kind people wear in kung fu movies, and wonder if he ever studied a martial art. Maybe he and Rose do tai chi exercises every morning, like the elderly people I saw in a park once in Chinatown, moving together with slow-motion grace.

It all makes me curious, but doesn't help me zero in on the right Secret Santa gift. I'll have to keep my eye out for clues.

But first, I've got a message to send. Destiny — and Dad — have answered my question.

I go into the locker room, take my phone out of my backpack, and send Amelia a text. It's two words, just four letters, but it says it all:

i'm in!

We've finally finished the last of the leftover turkey, so dinner tonight is tacos, a welcome relief.

I clean up the dishes in record time. I have homework from all but one of my teachers — I guess health class is good for *something* — plus midterms to study for, plus writing an opening paragraph for my English term paper, plus going over the solo I'll be rehearsing with Miss Bowman tomorrow. By the time Jess makes her nightly phone call, I feel as if I've been climbing a mountain.

Jess is in the same boat. She doesn't work after school, but *Snow Queen* rehearsals run until five-thirty. And she's got just as much homework as me, not to mention her text-happy prep school boyfriend. Apparently going out with Jason ("Fourth Jonas") Geissinger is almost a full-time job. Tonight, Jason texted her forty-nine times in one hour.

"Not fifty," says Jess. "Forty-nine. Isn't that wack?"

“Definitely,” I say, and before she can launch into the next isn’t-Jason-the-greatest monologue, I ask, “Did you do your opening paragraph for Mr. Amtzis?”

“I wrote *something*,” says Jess. “It’s just that I can’t keep my eyes open.”

“You and me both,” I say, stifling a yawn. And for maybe the third or fourth time in our lives, we say good night before either of our parents tells us to get ready for bed.

Chapter Three

The only thing worse than first-period health is first-period gym. I'm just never in the mood for sports so early in the morning.

But today, I have something to look forward to. Amelia is in my gym class. When I get to the locker room, she's already dressed in her track shorts and a Sky Blue FC jersey. She immediately throws her arms around me.

"You are my total hero for doing this," she says. "Your text made my night!"

"I didn't tell you the rest!" I say. "Guess what I tried on yesterday?"

"Um . . . clothes?" Amelia does not share my interest in fashion, unless it involves shoes with cleats.

"Your *Nutcracker* costume. They're having them cleaned at Cinderella."

"You're kidding!" Amelia says, delighted. "So, does it fit?"

"Like a glove," I say, pulling on my sweatpants and a waffle tee. There was no frost on the grass this morning, so Coach Ridley will probably make us warm up on the outdoor track.

"That's excellent," says Amelia. "Do you have ballet slippers?"

"Why would I have ballet slippers?" I ask.

"Good point. What's your shoe size?"

"Eight and a half," I tell her.

Amelia frowns. "I'm a seven. But hey, you know what? My mom wears an eight and a half. I'll grab one of her old pairs. She's got about twelve. Come on, let me show you the dance steps."

She moves into a stiff-armed pose, with her feet splayed and head cocked to one side. "This is the starting position."

"Like this?" I say, trying to mirror her arms.

"Ballet wrists," she says, adjusting my hands. "Here, like this. Feet are in second position."

Second position . . . which one is that? I have an unfortunate memory from my long-ago ballet classes, when the teacher showed all of us how to do knee bends called pliés. I did the first four positions like everyone else, but when I got into fifth, I couldn't bend without my knees banging into each other. The teacher came down the line to see what the problem was and realized I had my feet backward, with the toes facing inward instead of out. Everyone cracked up, and from then on my nickname was Sixth Position.

No wonder I quit.

I look at Amelia's feet, trying to imitate her.

"There you go," she says. "Then the toy maker comes up behind and winds me, once, twice, and I go like this." She cocks her head upward and moves her limbs with stiff precision, just like a mechanical doll. I don't care what she says about hating ballet, she's good. *Really* good.

Just then Kayleigh and two of the other cheerleaders, Savannah and Brandy, spot us.

"Hey, look!" says Savannah, "Attack of the robo-nerds!" She jogs Brandy's arm, giggling at her own joke, but Brandy looks over at Kayleigh to see how she's supposed to respond.

Kayleigh just tosses her blond ponytail and keeps walking, so Brandy does likewise. Savannah trails after them, saying glumly, "*I* thought it was funny."

Coach Ridley does drag us all out to the track, where it's cold enough to see our breath making puffy clouds. As we're walking and jogging alternate laps, Amelia does her best to describe her dance, occasionally demonstrating an arm or hand movement.

"You see?" she keeps saying, and I pant back, "Yeah, I *see*, but . . ." There's no way on earth I'm going to retain anything Amelia shows me while we circle the track with our gym class.

Finally, Coach Ridley blows her whistle. "Already?" Amelia says. She's used to chasing a soccer ball for hours and would run around the track all day long if they'd let her, but I'm feeling winded. My cheeks are stretched tight from the cold.

"So did you get any of that?" asks Amelia as we head back into the locker room.

"Maybe a little bit," I answer, catching my breath. "But I'm definitely going to need to rehearse it with you one-on-one."

"Okay, when?" says Amelia.

Good point. I shrug. "I work every day after school, and you've got ballet rehearsals every night, right?"

"Unfortunately, correct," sighs Amelia.

"Well, we've got math together, but somehow I don't think Mr. Perotta would go for us practicing dance steps. Much as I'd rather do that than geometry."

"How about lunch?" asks Amelia.

"Maybe, but not today." I grin at the thought. "I'm already booked."

Jess meets me in front of my locker as I'm changing textbooks for afternoon classes as fast as I can. My lunch bag sits ignored on the shelf.

"Sad news," she says mournfully, reaching into her lunch bag to show me a small ziplock of candy corn and sugar pumpkins. "Last of the Halloween candy stash till next year. You forgot your lunch," she adds as I close my locker.

"No time. I'll eat it on the bus after school," I tell her. "I'm meeting Miss Bowman to work on my solo."

"Oh, right," she says. "Well, break a — a what?" Jess and I have a silly tradition of putting other words that start with *L* in place of the usual backstage saying "Break a leg." But she seems to be temporarily out of ideas.

"Duh," I say, smacking my forehead. "Break a *lunch*."

"Good one," Jess grins.

My solo is *hard*. Even though I've got the practice CD, there's nothing like doing it live and in person. Ms. Wyant's here, too, so we'll work on my character as well as the music. Just seeing my drama advisor's bright smile and purple-framed glasses puts me more at ease.

"Why don't you just sing it once through as yourself — not in character, just to warm up," she instructs me. I nod, and she signals Miss Bowman to start playing. In spite of Ms. Wyant's reassuring words, I can feel my throat clenching a little with nervousness. I want so much to be good in this part.

To calm myself, I look around the familiar space as I'm singing. The music room is right next to the school auditorium, so it doubles as our backstage greenroom for Drama Club shows. It's where everyone does pre-show warmups and waits during scenes they're not in, listening for cues on the intercom. I can't look at those canvas-draped kettledrums and shelves full of instrument cases without getting a flutter of stage fright excitement.

Eleven days from today, I'll be back here with the rest of the cast, waiting to make my entrance in front of an actual audience.

To go out and sing this impossible song.

All *alone*.

I try to remind myself how flattered I was by the thought of a solo, but all I can think as I push my voice up for the last high note is, *Help!*

"Good start, Diana," Miss Bowman says from her piano stool. She probably means this as a compliment, but my heart sinks. "Good start" is not what you want to hear two weeks before you perform something difficult. I glance at Ms. Wyant, hoping to get some encouragement. But she just nods.

Miss Bowman goes over a phrase with me several times, correcting my rhythm. "You see where the stress is?" she says, picking the notes out on the keyboard. "It's one, two, then triplets — '*ta-da, ta DA-da. Winter snow FALL-ing.*' Repeat it with me."

I do. Her correction is simple, but I still stumble. "I'm sorry," I mumble on our third time through.

"Don't be sorry," she tells me. "You nailed it. '*Winter snow FALL-ing.*' "

"How old do you think the Enchantress is?" Ms. Wyant asks me.

I'm surprised but pleased by the question. "The script calls her ageless," I answer, but she shakes her head.

"Can't play 'ageless,' " she says. "Maybe she's been alive for a hundred years, but is she a wrinkled old crone or someone preserved at the peak of her beauty?"

"Like the Cullens in *Twilight*?" I ask. "Or Jesse in *Tuck Everlasting*."

"Exactly," Ms. Wyant says. "It's not how old she *is*, it's how old she appears. What do you think?"

I hesitate. If you had magic, why *wouldn't* you choose to be lovely and young for the rest of your life? On the other hand, if you had magic that was powerful enough to change summer to winter, but you couldn't change your own *face*, you'd be old and wrinkled and terribly bitter. Much more fun to act!

"I think she looks old," I say. "Ancient."

Ms. Wyant smiles. "Good. Well, then let's make her move that way, shall we?"

I nod eagerly. "Could I use a staff or a cane?"

"Great idea," she says, looking around the room. Her eyes fall on a push broom in the corner. "Try that broom handle."

I cross to get it, hearing muffled bits of melody from behind the doors of the practice rooms down the hall. I unscrew the broom handle from its wide base and start walking back with it. Ms. Wyant shakes her head.

"*Use* it," she says. "Rest your weight on it. Remember, your legs ache. It's hard to pick up your feet . . . your knees never straighten." As she narrates, I can feel my posture changing, my walk slowing down. I think of the way my grandmother moves when she's been on her feet too long.

"Short steps," says Ms. Wyant, watching me walk. "That's good. Now make your head heavy . . . let your shoulders hunch forward. Long arms. Your hands are stiff, they grip like claws."

I don't know what I look like as I cross the room, but I *feel* old and shrunken. If my costume includes a heavy cloak, it'll help me feel hunched. And I can't wear heels. For this character, I'll need something that shuffles, like slippers. When I get back to the piano, Ms. Wyant nods her approval. "By George, I think you've got it! Now let's make it sing."

As Miss Bowman starts playing the intro, Ms. Wyant gives me another adjustment that really helps. "Okay, now this time, you're old and you're *jealous*."

I nod, thinking of Kayleigh, who's playing the Snow Queen I'm singing about. I actually *am* a bit jealous that she got the lead, so it's easy to channel those feelings right into the song. The words kind of spit themselves out, and the high note becomes a cry of triumph.

"Excellent!" says Miss Bowman.

"Did you see how much that came to life?" says Ms. Wyant. "It's a song of revenge. Don't be afraid to get fierce with it."

I nod happily. Fierce, at Kayleigh? Sounds fun!

Ms. Wyant says, "Let's do it once more. I'm going to ask you to cross the room, moving in character, and then turn back and sing it to me from a distance. Look for a moment where you might get angry enough to raise up your staff. Okay?"

She signals Miss Bowman to start at the top. "Go," she says, and as the piano plays the introduction, I lean on my staff and start slowly across the room, turning back at the center to aim my song at Ms. Wyant.

The distance helps me to get up a good head of steam. Lifting my staff overhead, I hurl out the last high note.

Behind me, somebody says, "Cool!" I whirl around to see Will, who's just come out of a practice room, holding his silver euphonium.

In a split second I go from an ancient enchantress, angrily casting a spell of revenge, to a totally embarrassed thirteen-year-old girl who just got caught holding a broom handle over her head . . . and is turning bright red. Weirdly, Will looks just as embarrassed as I do — I don't think he meant to say "cool" out loud.

This helps a little, but I still feel like the world's biggest loser. "You heard that?" I ask, though the answer is obvious.

Will nods and mumbles, "You've got a great voice."

Well, at least he's turning kind of red, too. We could pass for a couple of McIntosh apples.

For the next two days, Amelia and I try to sneak ways to practice her *Nutcracker* dance steps in the locker room before gym class. Amelia also brings me a DVD of the Mikhail Baryshnikov version. "Ours is a lot shorter and the choreography is simpler, but you'll get to see the story, at least. Not to mention Baryshnikov."

"Wow!" I say, taking a look at the photos on the DVD cover. "Is your production's Nutcracker Prince this cute?"

"Gorgeous. Wait till you see him," Amelia grins. "He's Russian, too. Nikolai Chodoff. Zoe has a major — and I do mean *major* — crush on him. But he's actually married to this snooty Russian ballerina. I call her Diva Central."

By Wednesday, I'm feeling confident enough to do a command performance with Amelia in front of Jess and Sara. We're in the bathroom next to the cafeteria, dancing in front of a big mirror. It's clear that Amelia's an awful lot better than I am. "I totally stink," I moan.

"No, you don't," Jess says loyally. "I couldn't do that to save my life."

"It looks good," Sara says. "But you might want to work on your hands. Amelia's thumbs are at more of a right angle." Sara's grandmother is teaching her classical Indian dance, so it makes sense that she'd notice hand movements.

Amelia demonstrates. "It's the mechanical doll thing. You want to avoid any softness or curve."

"Like this?" I ask, holding my hands out more stiffly.

"Perfect!" says Jess.

"Much better," says Sara.

"You see?" says Amelia. "Throw a wig and some makeup on that, and you're set. Piece of cake."

Hardly. It's not just if I can pull off the dance, it's if I can pass myself off as Amelia backstage. Which means completely avoiding her mother, her sister, and all the dancers she's been rehearsing with for weeks.

Oh, yeah, and the little matter of making it to *The Snow Queen* on time, so I can be at my very best for opening night. Just thinking about it makes my stomach lurch.

The afternoon seems endless, with midterm reviews in every class, and I'm relieved when the bell finally rings.

But it doesn't feel right to go out to the bus after school when all my friends — not to mention Her Royal Kayleighness — are heading to *Snow Queen* rehearsals. I walk Jess to the auditorium door, where she's met by Ethan and Riley and heads down the center aisle, already laughing at something they said. I don't think she even realizes that she just left without saying good-bye to her best friend.

I watch cast members set down their backpacks and gather onstage, jostling and joking in front of the partly built set. I try to remind myself I'll be part of this happy crowd all next week, but I still feel left out.

And of course, as I'm turning to leave, I run smack into Kayleigh. She looks at me with puppy-dog eyes. "Don't you get to stay and rehearse with us yet?" she says, her voice dripping with phony sympathy.

I shake my head. "I have to work. But I'll be here next week."

Kayleigh nods and smiles. "Good thing it's such a small part."

I'm about to retaliate with something equally fake-nice, but Ms. Wyant comes up behind her. "Diana, I'm so glad

I caught you. Could you please show me a sketch for your costume design by tomorrow?"

I nod happily. "Nelson's going to work on it this afternoon."

Kayleigh asks, "Who's Nelson? Someone from the Laundromat?"

"It's a *cleaners*," I tell her. "And Nelson is —"

Jess must have remembered me after all, because she appears at that moment and jumps right in. "Nelson designs costumes for Tasha Kane and a new MTV show, okay?" she says.

"He's very cool," I say, smiling at Jess.

"The coolest," she says. "Too cool for this school. Tell him hi."

For once in her life, Kayleigh's totally speechless. "Later," I tell her, and grin all the way to the bus.

I can't wait to give Jess's greeting to Nelson, *and* see what he's thinking for my costume. Because of his TV show commitments, his hours often change at the last minute, but I'm still disappointed when I open the door to the Tailoring section and he isn't there. Loretta and Sadie both greet me warmly, and Loretta, who's sewing gold braid onto one of the *Nutcracker* costumes, gives me such a sly grin that I wonder if she might be my Secret Santa.

I walk back out past the twin frowns of Joyless and Lara and feel really grateful I don't have to be Secret Santa to either of *them*. There's a full cart of tagged clothes, and I roll it back into the workroom.

I'm going through the new garments on the sorting table when Cat arrives, breathless as always. "I'll tell you what I want for Christmas," she says, pinning her name tag onto her green smock. "A traffic dissolver. You point it at somebody's bumper, and *poof*, they're out of your way. I am so sick of punching in five minutes late every day."

"I don't think anyone blames you," I say.

"Red Audi? *Poof!* Garbage truck? Disappeared," says Cat, demonstrating her imaginary powers with a pointing forefinger.

"Would it work on people?" I ask her.

"Only mean ones," says Cat. "Oh, and homework. *Poof!*"

"I could use one of those this week," I tell her, setting aside a camel-hair coat with a chalk-circled stain. I carry it back to Rose Chen's workstation, slowing to look at her husband. There he is, dressed in the same white shirt and black pants as always, his white hair neatly combed as he sprays starch onto the French cuffs of a perfectly ironed tuxedo shirt.

Sad to say, I'm not picking up any hints for the perfect gift. (I guess I could buy him a new spray bottle, but that hardly seems very festive.)

I hand Rose the camel-hair coat. "Thank you," she says, peering over the top of her glasses at the stain.

"Of course," I say. "Hope it comes out."

"All comes out," she says, which sounds extra wise in her Chinese accent.

As I head back toward the sorting table, I'm thrilled to see Nelson standing with Cat. "You're here!" I cry.

"Last time I noticed," he says.

"I thought you were working with Ingrid today, on the show."

Nelson shakes his head. "Only show I'm planning to work on today is *The Nutcracker.* Can I steal you up front in the Tailoring section?"

"You bet," I grin happily.

Cat says, "Not fair! You go off and have all the fun, and I get stuck working with Lara and Joyless."

"If they give you trouble," I say, "just remember: *Poof! Poof!*"

"I'm not even going to ask," Nelson says as we walk toward the front. He tells Miss MacInerny, "I'm taking Diana to Tailoring for a few minutes."

Before she can answer, we're through the glass door. That's the way Nelson does things. He doesn't fuss about asking permission, he just makes it happen.

He's lined up a series of tasks for me, fastening trim onto tutus and whipstitching hems. I know he could do it himself in a third of the time — so could Loretta and Sadie — but I'm not complaining. One of my favorite perks of working at Cinderella Cleaners is the sewing and tailoring lessons I've gotten from Nelson. Plus this is the type of work you can do while you talk.

I tell him what Jess said to Kayleigh, which makes him laugh. "That Jess is a pistol," he says. "It's a redhead thing."

This would be a perfect chance to ask him about my costume for the show, but it feels kind of pushy. Still, Ms.

Wyant asked me to show her a drawing tomorrow. I take a deep breath.

"I know you've been incredibly busy," I start, "but I wondered if you've had a chance to think about, you know, my Enchantress costume at all."

"Yes, I have," Nelson says calmly. "And I've decided I'm not going to design it."

Oh, no!

"You're not?" I ask in a quivering voice.

Nelson shakes his head, looking me right in the eye. "*You* are."

Chapter Four

My mouth must have dropped wide open, because Nelson starts laughing. "You're going to catch flies in that thing!"

"*I'm* designing my costume?" I stammer.

"Why not?" he says. "You showed me your sketches, you've got great ideas. You're already learning the sewing skills, and if you need help cutting your pattern, I'll be your mentor. Just call me Tim Gunn."

"You really think I could do this?" I ask.

"Absolutely," says Nelson. "I don't work with amateurs."

I'm beyond flattered, but I ask Nelson when I'd have the time.

"No time like the present," he answers. "Let's take a look at those sketches."

"Nelson, I'm supposed to be working!"

"You *are* working," he shrugs. "I asked if I could have your help in Tailoring today, and I'm giving you an assignment."

A *super* assignment! I'm thrilled. But I'm also a little embarrassed. Nelson's design sketches are so professional, and mine are just . . . doodles. He spreads them out on the cutting table and studies the various looks. "Tell me who your character is," he says. " 'Cause I'm getting a lot of different messages."

"When I did these, I didn't quite know," I admit. "But the way it's evolved, she's old, very powerful, and kind of bitter."

"Well, I'm liking the cloak," Nelson says. "Heavy fabric to weigh you down. It'll help age you."

"Exactly," I say. "That's what we've been working on. And I'll have a long staff."

"Very Gandalf," he nods. "You should wear something high-necked and simple beneath it. Long skinny black arms, like Cruella De Vil. And we'll work up some kind of a winter-themed headdress, like this icicle one you drew here. That sound good?"

Gandalf plus Cruella De Vil, with an icicle headdress? "Sounds sensational!" I tell him, beaming from ear to ear.

Nelson says, "Let's go shopping!"

Walking into a fabric store with Nelson Martinez is like going into the world's best buffet when you're really hungry. He does have an actual errand — buying replacement buttons and trim for *The Nutcracker*'s soldier costumes — but as soon as he's scooped all those into a basket, we head for the fabric racks to find the Enchantress's cloak.

There are shelves stuffed full of long rolls, and tables piled with flat bolts in all textures and colors. We start out with the velvets and velveteens, which are arrayed like a rainbow. Some of the colors are gorgeous — I'm especially drawn to a rich blue with lavender tones — but they feel more royal than magical crone.

"What do you think?" Nelson says.

"I think I'd like something with more of a texture," I answer.

He nods as if that were the answer he'd hoped for. "Let's try the brocades and satins," he says. "Over there."

We browse through a dizzying display of fabrics. Some have geometrical or floral patterns — too intricate. Others look too modern.

"Are you starting to narrow it down?" Nelson asks, and I realize with a guilty start that we're taking a *very* long time on this errand.

"I guess . . . well, there's that lavender satin we both kind of liked."

"But didn't love," Nelson points out.

"Or that crinkled metallic blue. What do you think?"

"It's the designer's choice," Nelson says.

Indecisive, I scan the racks one last time, just in case I missed something. And like magic, my eye is drawn upward to a long roll on the very top shelf. It's an enchanted silvery blue, the exact color moonlight would be if it came in cloth form, shot through with uneven streaks of ice white and blue gray.

"There," I point. Nelson looks up and his smile widens.

"I knew it," he says. "You've got the eye, Diana Donato."

He climbs up on one of the ladders and pulls the roll out of the rack. A frowning employee comes toward us. "Excuse me . . ." she starts, but when Nelson turns, her face relaxes. "Oh, it's *you*," she says. "No rules for Nelson Martinez. Make yourself right at home."

"Thanks, Roseanne," Nelson says with a wink. He shoulders the roll and steps down to the floor, unrolling a half yard or so. "You like it?"

I nod. *Like* isn't the word — I adore it.

Nelson runs his fingers over it. "Nice hand," he says. "It's got some weight, ought to take stage light well. Go on, give it a touch."

I do. It's just perfect. I nod again.

"Speechless," says Nelson. "Now that's a good sign."

"I *love* it," I blurt.

Nelson smiles. "So let's grab your gown fabric, and maybe a hit of faux fur for the collar. I clocked a few choices while you were browsing." He leads me to another bolt rack, and my eye goes straight to a stretchy dark fabric that looks almost black but is actually deep midnight blue.

"How about that one?" I ask.

"Same one I picked. Great minds think alike." He lifts up that bolt, too, holding it next to the cloak fabric.

"Can I help?" I ask him.

"Please," Nelson says. "That's like asking a waitress at Sam's Diner if she needs help carrying two breakfast specials. Here's your fun furs. I would steer you away from the faux leopard print, but other than that . . ."

I point. "That one."

It's a thick plushy white with a light frost of black at the tips, like a snowshoe hare. Nelson grins even wider. "We're three for three."

He shoulders the third bolt and says, "So? Do they work with each other?"

"Absolutely!" I say. If I squint, I can practically see the whole outfit.

Nelson leads me to the cutting table, where the woman he called Roseanne gives him a big flirty smile. Only then do I get a look at the price of the cloak fabric, scrawled onto one end of the roll.

"Nelson, I can't afford this!" I gasp.

"You don't have to," he says. "It's on me."

"That's ridiculous," I protest. "You can't do that!"

"Try and stop me," says Nelson, laying the roll in front of Roseanne. "Two and a half yards."

"This is totally over the top," I say.

He raises his eyebrows. "That's the way I roll. A, I get a professional discount. B, it's Christmas."

My eyes open wide. "Are you my Secret Santa?" I ask him.

"I wish," Nelson says. "You'd be fun."

"Tell me you didn't get Lara, or Miss MacInerny!"

"It's called *Secret* Santa," he says. "So my lips are sealed."

When Jess calls me before bed, I leap for the phone. For the first time in ages, I don't have to steel myself for the nightly outpouring of Jason updates and rehearsal gossip. I have news of my own.

"Guess what Nelson did?" I blurt out. And before Jess has a chance to guess, I tell her the whole story.

"That's unbelievable," Jess says. She sounds just as excited as I am. "I wish I had a Nelson. The costume crew's basically just recycling old costumes from other shows and adding cheap crowns. I wouldn't be surprised if someone winds up wearing the overalls from *Our Town* plus a rhinestone tiara."

"Well, what about your Jester costume?" I ask.

"Undetermined as yet. I'm stressing," Jess says.

Suddenly an inspiration strikes. "Ethan's clown suit!" I say, remembering the costume that Kayleigh's parents special-ordered for the masquerade ball, back in the dark days when Ethan and Kayleigh were going out.

"What about it?" says Jess.

"Maybe you could wear it." There's a stone silence on Jess's end. "You know . . . clown, jester? It does look kind of medieval. And it was sewn by Nelson. Okay, you're not saying anything. Bad idea?"

"I'm doing my best not to think about putting a garment on me that came off of E. T. Horowitz, alien boy," says Jess.

"Jess, he wore it last *month*!"

"Even so," says Jess. "If Ethan wore it, it should go into quarantine. Not onto me." She pauses a second. "You think he still has it?"

"Ask him," I say. "You see him every day."

"Sadly true," she says. "Wouldn't it be great if Jason could swap schools with Ethan? Then I'd see *him* every day." I can't help rolling my eyes. Here comes the part where she bends my ear for the next half hour about the latest text messages from her preppy prince.

I stretch out on my bed, settling in for the monologue. It's a good thing I love Jess so much. If she weren't my best friend since forever, this really could be hard to take.

But a few minutes in, she throws a surprise question at me. "So what kind of Christmas gift are you supposed to get for your boyfriend?"

"How should I know?"

"Because Jason is sure to pick out something really expensive," Jess says, sounding worried. "What should I give *him*? What are you giving Will?"

Whoa! "That isn't the same thing, Jess. Will isn't my *boyfriend*."

Jess lets out a deep sigh. "Oh, come on, are you really still playing this game? Enough is enough! One of you *has* to say something official. Or I will!"

"Don't you dare," I say, sitting bolt upright.

"I won't if you get to it first," says Jess. "Call it the Great B-Word Challenge."

"B-Word as in . . . ?"

"Boyfriend," says Jess. "I double-dog dare you."

At lunch the next day, I keep looking at Will, mentally trying to form the word *boyfriend. My boyfriend.* Why does that phrase seem so *impossible*?

Will looks up and meets my eye, and I feel myself blushing, as if he could read the thoughts inside my head the same way I can read IRON AND WINE on his T-shirt.

"Are you singing today?" he asks.

I shake my head. "Not till Friday. Miss Bowman is only free two days a week. I wish I had more practice time with the piano, but those are all the lunch slots she's got."

"I play piano a bit," mumbles Will. "If the practice room's free."

I can feel myself beaming. "You do?"

We finish our lunches in record time and walk down the hall to the music room. Will's hands are jammed deep in his pockets, and I'm much too aware of the distance between us. He seems to be walking a little too close to the lockers on his side. I look down at the red and green holiday laces I put in my Converses, feeling like a total geek.

"So how many instruments do you actually play?" I ask Will. Maybe I can get him to talk about music.

"You mean *well*?" says Will. "Bass. And euphonium, sort of."

"And piano," I prompt him.

"I don't play piano that well," he says. "Just enough to read music."

"That's way better than me," I say.

"Did you ever play an instrument?" Will asks me, and I shake my head.

"My mom wanted me to take piano," I say. "But it just never happened."

"Why not?"

I pause. Should I tell him the truth, or will it be too awkward? The truth, I decide. "She got sick," I say simply. "But maybe someday."

Will nods. He doesn't say anything, but I can tell he's thinking about what I just told him, not trying to hide from it. This makes me feel closer to him. I bet Mom would have liked him. A lot.

We've arrived at the music room, which is empty except for the sound of a flute from behind a practice room door. Will sits down on the piano bench and lifts up the cover to reveal the keyboard.

"Do you have the music?" he asks, pushing his floppy dark bangs off his forehead. I reach into my backpack and take out the sheet music, setting it onto the piano. My arm nearly brushes his shoulder.

"Cool," he says, scanning the pages and playing a couple of notes. "Do you want to sit or stand?"

I've always practiced my song standing up, but I'd be embarrassed to pick up the broom handle and do all the movements in front of Will. And I'm not going to lie. I like the idea of sitting with him on the piano bench.

"I guess . . . sit," I say, and he slides over for me. We sit side by side on the bench, being careful not to let our legs touch. Will takes a deep breath and leans forward, lifting his hands to the keyboard. He's not as smooth as Miss Bowman, but he makes his way through the intro. And now it's my turn to — help! — *sing*.

I start out very softly, both because I'm self-conscious and because I don't want to blast Will in the eardrum. But as the song builds, both Will and I get more confident. I even manage to hit my high note without my voice cracking.

"You sounded great," says Will, turning toward me. My breath catches.

"You, too," I say, meeting his eyes. If this were a movie with grown-ups playing us, this is the moment where the two characters would lean forward and kiss. But after a heart-racing moment, we both look away, feeling kind of embarrassed and very thirteen.

Chapter Five

I don't know whether it's my close call or the holiday season, but suddenly I start seeing people kissing everywhere. At the Christmas tree stand I pass on the ride to work, a couple is getting cozy under hanging mistletoe. And when I get off the bus, I see Cat leaning through the open window of her boyfriend's van to kiss him good-bye.

Two kisses in two minutes! Tell me that isn't insane!

I hang up my coat and report to Miss MacInerny. But Nelson intercepts me. "I'm claiming Diana again. I need two more hands on the *Nutcracker* order."

"You should have this finished by now," Lara says. Her eyes flash angrily. Why is it any of her business?

"Yes, I know," Nelson says mildly. "That's why I need two more hands, so we'll finish today."

Lara mutters something in Russian, but Joyless agrees to Nelson's request. Feeling like the luckiest girl in the world, I follow him to Tailoring.

Sadie and Loretta are both fixing costumes. I recognize the green cape belonging to Herr Drosselmeyer and the oversize hoopskirt of Mother Ginger. But I can't remember the rest of the *Nutcracker* characters. I make a mental note to watch Amelia's DVD this weekend.

Nelson's refreshing a few shredding tutus with yards of fresh tulle. He gives me the task of replacing frayed lace on the Spanish dancer costumes and hot-gluing some missing jewels onto the Mouse King's head mask and crown. The long rodent nose and hollow eyes give me a shudder, but it's kind of fun.

After I've squared that away, I ask Nelson what's next.

"How about the Enchantress's cloak?" he suggests.

"During work hours?" I ask, concerned.

"Hey, it's a costume," Nelson says with a shrug. "We just finished the *Nutcracker* order, but who's going to know?"

I look at the glass door, a bit worried. What if Lara or Joyless comes in?

"Diana, your show is next weekend, hello. But if you would rather roll carts to the workroom for Miss MacInerny . . ." says Nelson.

Okay, well, no contest. Especially since I'll have rehearsals next week and won't be at the cleaners. I have today, tomorrow, and Saturday, and that is *it*.

I take a deep breath, reminding myself not to panic.

The cloak is pretty simple to cut, and Nelson shows me how to lay out pattern pieces to make the least waste. "I'll help you with shaping the shoulders and collar," he says. "Other than that, it's just hems. You could sew this in your sleep."

He hands me a pair of pinking shears, and I get to work. I love the texture and sheen of the fabric, and as I'm working, I imagine myself wearing this cloak and coming offstage after the last curtain call. Filled with joy, I glide into the music room backstage, where everyone's hugging each other . . . and then I see Will, with his sound crew headphones still around his neck, standing next to the piano bench where we sat side by side, and —

"Diana?" Nelson snaps his fingers in front of my face. "Earth to daydreamer."

"I wasn't . . ." I start, but he raises his eyebrows and looks at me.

"Let me guess. Is he tall, with nice eyes that his hair's always falling in front of?"

I sputter. Nelson can seem kind of psychic sometimes, but how in the *world* would he know I was picturing Will? They *have* met each other, when Will's father was working on Tasha Kane's video with Nelson, but that was a while ago.

"What makes you think I'm . . . whatever you think?" I say, totally flustered.

"Just a wild guess," Nelson smirks. "I ran into young Will at the ShopRite the other day, and as soon as I mentioned your name, he got the same look in his eye."

"He did *not*!" I exclaim.

"Fine," Nelson sniffs. "I guess you're the one who was there, not me." He goes to the thread rack and takes down a spool that perfectly matches the cool moonlit blue of my fabric. Meanwhile, I can't stop smiling.

Thursday and Friday are so crazy busy I'm actually starting to feel like a windup doll. My friends are also fried at the edges — especially Amelia: Her opening night for *The Nutcracker* is next Thursday, two days before *The Snow Queen*'s.

"Six days from today," she moans over lunch. "*Five* performances. Thursday night, Friday night, *two* shows on Saturday, Sunday matinee. I tell you, this soccer camp better be worth it."

For me, too, I think.

"It totally is," Sara promises. "You're going to love it."

"I wish *we* could have five performances," Riley says. "It seems crazy to do all this work and then have it be over so quickly. Saturday night, Sunday afternoon, bam."

"If we're doing wishes," says Ethan, "I wish we could jump straight to winter break."

"Amen!" says Amelia. "And soccer camp."

I'll pass on the soccer, but vacation is starting to sound pretty heavenly.

Fay's stressing, too, and dinner on Friday is take-out Chinese. The twins are delighted and so am I — no pots and pans for me to wash! After I finish tossing out soggy cartons, Dad asks for my help hanging icicle lights on the front of the house.

"I could manage alone," he says. "But it's simpler with two. Not to mention much friendlier."

"Sure," I nod, glad to spend time with him.

I carry the lights and a couple of outdoor extension cords, and Dad gets his housepainter's stepladder out of the basement. The air's clear and frosty, and there's a bright sliver of moon.

"Listen," says Dad, pointing upward. At first I don't know what he means. Then somewhere high overhead I hear Canada geese honking.

"Heading south for the winter," says Dad. "I'm surprised they're flying so late."

We both stand still, listening to the distant wild sound. It reminds me of feeding the geese at the pond near the farm stand when I was little. Mom used to crumble up stale ends of bread and keep them in the freezer for our expeditions. I glance at Dad, wondering if I should say anything, but decide it would make him too sad.

He sets up the ladder and climbs it without hesitation, like the housepainter he used to be. I hand up the first string of lights, and he starts clipping them to the gutter. "Have you thought of a present for Ashley and Brynna?" he asks me.

"Not really." This isn't the heart-to-heart I had in mind.

"I hope you can find something special," he says, stretching to reach the next clip. "They're so happy to have a big sister."

Where is he getting this wacko idea that Ashley and Brynna can stand me? It certainly isn't from anything *I* said. But I don't want Dad to feel bad, so I just say, "I will."

"Thank you," says Dad, and I hand him the next string of lights. He looks up at the geese. "I miss her so much at this time of year," he says softly.

"Me, too," I tell him, and we don't have to say any more.

After I've run through my solo, practiced my doll dance, and worked on my English term paper until my eyes start to cross, I head downstairs with the DVD Amelia gave me. I'm fully expecting someone to be watching TV, in which case I'll have to make do with my laptop's small screen. But to my surprise, Dad, Fay, and the twins are all playing Disney Monopoly. It figures Fay would pick a real estate game.

"Okay if I watch this?" I ask, holding up the DVD.

"What is it?" asks Fay.

"*The Nutcracker.* Something Amelia is in," I say, sliding the disc in the player and hoping my anxious expression won't give me away.

"Amelia's in a movie?" asks Brynna, impressed.

"She's doing it with her sister's ballet school." *And so am I,* I add silently. "The movie version has professional dancers."

"Oh," Brynna says, losing interest immediately. I press PLAY and sit down on the couch. In spite of how tired I am, I'm swept up in the story immediately.

Clara and Fritz's parents are having a big Christmas party, and the mysterious toy maker Herr Drosselmeyer arrives with magical presents, including . . . a life-size mechanical doll.

Hey, that's Amelia! That's *me*!

I sit forward to watch.

"This is *boring*," groans Ashley. "Watch something with words."

"I like it," I say, eyes glued to the doll dancer. She's really good. And she's doing the same dance I'll have to swan-fake. A *long* dance. I'm so glad ours is shorter — and that Amelia and I finally got to make plans for a real rehearsal at her house this Sunday.

"The music's great," says Dad.

The next scene is Clara's dream. The clock strikes midnight, and suddenly the room is full of enormous mice! The toy soldiers come to life and start fighting them, led by the Nutcracker, who's magically grown to full size and become an *incredible* dancer.

At this point I notice the twins are both watching, ignoring their board game. Fay starts to hand Brynna the dice, saying, "Your turn," but Dad raises his finger to his lips.

Ashley is first to get out of her seat and join me on the couch, but Brynna follows soon after. The three of us sit side by side, watching enraptured as Clara throws a shoe at the Mouse King, saving the day. As the mice carry him off, the Nutcracker turns into a handsome prince and starts dancing with Clara. Beautifully.

"Wow," Brynna breathes. I would have to agree.

"Look at our three girls together," Dad says happily. Fay goes to her purse and takes out the digital camera she uses to photograph houses she's selling.

"That's our holiday e-card," she says. "Everyone smile."

We do, and for once I feel almost glad I'm a sort-of big sister. Then Fay says, "If you girls like watching ballet, why don't we all go see Amelia perform? There are posters all over town. It's next weekend, isn't it?"

NO!!! I want to scream. But somehow I manage to keep my cool. "Next weekend is *The Snow Queen*," I say quickly. "I hope you're all coming to that."

"Wouldn't miss it," Dad beams. "We'll be there on Saturday, opening night."

But Fay isn't done. "Doesn't *The Nutcracker* have matinees? We could see it on Sunday afternoon."

"No, we can't," Ashley pipes up. "We're going skating with Marissa on Sunday."

"Oh, that's right," Fay says. "Well, then, what about Saturday?"

This isn't happening! My heart's climbing into my throat, but I give myself acting notes. *Calm. Stay calm. At least sound calm.* "I have an early rehearsal that day," I tell Fay, hoping she won't say, "Then we'll go without you." They *cannot* see the Saturday matinee of *The Nutcracker*!

Luckily, I have a couple of unexpected allies. "Two shows in one day is too much," Ashley says.

"Totally," Brynna says, folding her arms.

I'm so relieved that I hear myself blurt out, "I'm going with Sara and Jess Thursday night, if you two want to come."

Dad looks really pleased. "Well, that sounds just perfect, Diana. What a lovely offer!" He gives Fay a "there, you see?" look.

"Terrific," she says. "I'll buy us all tickets."

"I can't join you on Thursday night," Dad says, and my heart dips again. If Fay has to choose between him and me, she's sure to choose him. *Please, not the Saturday matinee!* But Dad adds, "Why don't you all make it a ladies' night out?"

I hold my breath. Not that a ladies' night out with the twins and my stepmother sounds like my fantasy outing, but at least they'll be watching Amelia, not *me.*

Fay sighs and says, "Fine," and Dad winks at me. It's easy to see what's on his Christmas wish list. He's trying to make us all get along better.

Chapter Six

Saturday is our busiest day yet at the cleaners. The Fleet Feet Dancers' van comes to pick up the whole order of *Nutcracker* costumes, including the harlequin doll dress that Nelson fitted with elasticized gussets so it'll fit both Amelia and me.

So many customers come in with drop-offs that there's an actual traffic jam in the parking lot, and they all seem to need special care or emergency one-hour service. I see what Dad meant about this time of year. The pace is so frantic I actually feel guilty about taking next week off for rehearsals.

Of course I don't have a spare minute to work on my Enchantress costume. I have finished sewing the cloak, which was mostly just hemming, but the gown's still pinned to the pattern pieces Nelson made from my sketch, and we haven't even started to work on the headdress. "Don't worry," says Nelson. "You created the look, and I'll do the rest of the sewing. I've got your back."

Sunday isn't much better. Fay is showing a condo she hopes to unload in this calendar year, so we speed through our usual brunch tradition. This is fine with me, since I'm supposed to "study math" with Amelia (aka sneak a ballet rehearsal!) before she meets her mother and Zoe at Fleet Feet. Then I'm going to Jess's to cram for our Monday biology midterm.

Not what you'd call a relaxing weekend.

Amelia meets me at the door with a loud "Did you bring your math textbook?" so I guess that Zoe and Mrs. Williams haven't left yet. We sit at the kitchen table, going over equations while they buzz around us like dragonflies, scooping up toe shoes, water bottles, and dance bags. At long last, they get into their car, and Amelia slams her textbook shut. "That's enough of *that*."

All very well for her — she does math puzzles for fun — but I actually *do* need to prep for our midterm.

"Later," Amelia says when I bring this up. "Dad'll be back home for lunch, so let's get the ballet stuff out of the way while there's nobody home."

I'm all for that, so we head for the bedroom she shares with her sister. It's almost a joke how different the two halves of the room look. You might think ballerinas are neat and soccer players are messy, but you would be wrong, at least in this family. Zoe's side is a blizzard of tutus, scarves, toe shoes, and magazines, with pink scatter pillows and a striped bedspread twisting down onto the floor. Amelia's side looks like a monk could move in, with the bed tightly made and nothing at all on the walls. The only decor is a row of trophies, arranged in a gleaming V on the windowsill.

She goes right to her bureau and pulls out a drawer in which every garment is folded in perfect squares. "Let's get you dressed," she says, handing over a pastel pink leotard.

"I don't need to wear this," I protest.

"Oh, yeah?" says Amelia. "Try doing a leg lift in skinny jeans."

Oops. I didn't think of that.

"Besides," she continues, "you're trying to look just like me. If we're both ballet clones, there'll be no distractions. Here, try these on. They're an eight and a half." She hands me an old pair of ballet slippers.

We put on the pink leotards, adding tutus to mimic the flaring skirt of the harlequin doll costume. Getting dressed side by side feels familiar, as if we're both standing in front of our gym lockers. My ballet slippers are just a bit tight, which Amelia assures me is perfect. "You *don't* want them to flop off your feet, trust me," she says grimly.

We twist our hair back into buns and look at ourselves in the mirror. It's not a bad match. We're close to the same height, and we both have brown eyes. Amelia's shoulders and back are much stronger than mine, but the poufy sleeves of the doll dress should cover the difference.

Amelia talks me through the whole scene — how the boy doll and I will be hidden in giant gift boxes, how Drosselmeyer will mime winding the key on my back, I'll do my dance, and then freeze in place while the boy does his jumping jack dance.

"His name's Eli," Amelia says, making a face as she cues up the music on her laptop. "Mega-nerd."

She lifts her arms into the now-familiar position, and I do the same. We run through the dance steps so many times I feel ready to drop.

Then Amelia says, "Just do it once more without following me. I'll be Drosselmeyer and wind you up." She cues up the music one more time, and I do my best.

Which is honestly not good enough. As I'm "winding down," I turn left where I should have turned right and wind up with my legs in a pretzel. Sixth Position returns!

Amelia studies me. "Okay, well, you've got the gist," she says, not too convincingly. "Besides, you've got six days to practice."

Just shoot me.

The only good thing about dancing ballet is it makes other things that scare you to death, like biology midterms, seem like a piece of cake. Jess and I get right to work, and we study nonstop until four o'clock, when Mrs. Munson knocks on Jess's door and announces it's time to go pick out a Christmas tree.

Jess looks at me. "You're coming with us, right?"

I hesitate, torn. I still have to study for French, but that test's not till Tuesday. Besides, I love picking out trees, and since Fay bought a white artificial one that gets stored in our basement all year, it just isn't the same.

"I guess so," I say. "As long as we're back before dinner."

"I'm working the night shift," says Mrs. Munson, "so that is a guarantee."

We pile into the Munsons' old Subaru wagon, with Jess's kid brother, Dash, clamoring, "I get the front seat." We drive out to Davenport's Farm Stand. Half of the parking lot's covered with wooden tree racks, and the smell of cut pine is delicious. Jess and I head in one direction and Mrs. Munson and Dash in the other. We can hear his shouts of "How about this one? No, *this* one!" across the whole lot.

"When are you decorating your tree?" asks Jess.

"Christmas Eve," I say. "And all of Fay's ornaments match, so it isn't much fun." I miss the old days, when Mom and Dad and I hung up a mismatched assortment of old-fashioned doodads and glittery snowflakes I made in preschool.

Jess nods, and I know she knows just what I mean. "Did you find the right present for Jason?" I ask her.

"I'm going to make us matching friendship bracelets in his favorite colors: blue, tan, and maroon," Jess says. "What do you think, will he like that?"

I'm not so sure Jason's a friendship bracelet kind of guy, but I don't want Jess to worry, so I tell her, "That's great. He'll love that you made it yourself." Which is probably true, even if he won't wear it with his Foreman Academy uniform and Ralph Lauren loafers.

We've come to the end of the lot, where bundled-up guys are passing a tree through a loop that flattens the branches down and wraps it inside a mesh net. There's a chopping block a few yards away where they cut off the oversize bottom branches that get in the way of a tree stand. I look at the discarded branches and get an idea.

"What do you do with those leftover branches?" I ask one of the workers as his buddy shoulders the wrapped tree and lugs it to the roof rack of somebody's car.

He shrugs. "Use 'em for mulch. If you want 'em, they're yours."

"Cool!" I say, kneeling to gather some sweet-smelling pine boughs.

Jess looks at me like I might have just lost my mind. "What are you going to do with mulch?"

I shake my head. "I'm going to make my own mini tree. For my room."

The next few days are a blur of midterms and tech week. The set still isn't finished, and most of the cast hasn't quite learned their lines. The first time I get up to sing my solo, still using a broom handle for my magic staff (note to self: Talk to the props crew!), Kayleigh sits in the front row of the auditorium with her arms folded, as if she's daring me to miss my high note.

So of course I do. Miss Bowman gives me a supportive smile, and so does Will, who's noting down sound cues. But Kayleigh looks pleased, and I slink offstage, feeling like a loser. I've got to do better on opening night!

In spite of the pressure, I *am* thrilled to be going to Drama Club rehearsals. The stage manager is a tiny Asian-American girl named Gracie Chen, who bustles around making sure we sign in on her clipboard.

On Wednesday, she's wearing her hair piled on top of her head in a loose bun, secured with a beautiful pair of red and black lacquered chopsticks. "Those are gorgeous," I tell her. "Where did you find them?"

"My grandfather collects fancy chopsticks," she says, putting a check by my name. All of a sudden, her last name clicks in my head. I wonder if she might be related to Li Chen, my Secret Santa recipient? I know it's a common Chinese name, but it's worth a try.

"Gracie?" I venture. "Do you know a couple named Li and Rose Chen who work at Cinderella Cleaners?"

Gracie peers at me over the rim of her cute tortoiseshell glasses. "Of course. They're my grandparents. I thought you knew that."

"That is so cool!" I tell her. "They're both really nice."

And Li Chen collects chopsticks! Solved *that* Santa problem!

Beaming ear to ear, I sit down next to Jess, who's finishing up the most intricate friendship bracelet I've ever seen. It's almost an inch wide, with a herringbone pattern and all kinds of complicated internal twists.

"That's amazing!" I tell her. "Jason's going to love it!"

"I hope so," she says, tying knot after knot.

Ms. Wyant walks onto the stage to address us. "All right," she says. "Time to get serious. Today's our last run-through, tomorrow is stop tech, and Friday is our dress rehearsal. That's it, people. That's all we've got. So as of today, no more asking for cues. If you forget your line, improvise — that's what you'll have to do if it happens in front of an audience. Better yet, don't let it happen. Whenever you're not in a scene, find a partner, go out in the hall, and run, run, run your lines. Got it?"

"We've got it!" yells Ethan, and everyone nods and says, "Got it."

"All right," says Ms. Wyant. "Everyone up here for warm-ups."

Jess sets down her friendship bracelet, securing the end with a pin, and we both hurry onto the stage, ready to start our familiar routine of stretches and voice exercises. For the next three hours, we don't have to think about anything else in the world but *The Snow Queen*. What a relief!

I'm in my bedroom, working away on my English paper that seems to get stupider with every sentence. Why haven't

I *finished* it yet? I'm beating myself up so much I can't think straight, which of course makes it even harder to write a good sentence. *I'll never get out of this quicksand*, I think. *I am doomed.*

The phone ring surprises me. It's too early for Jess, and I can't afford a distraction right now. Not that I'm getting anything done, but . . .

"Hello?" I answer.

"Diana?" Could that voice, low and strangled, be *Jess*? "Jason dumped me," she sobs. "By *text message*!"

"You're kidding." I sit on the edge of my bed.

"Do I sound like I'm kidding?" says Jess, and I have to admit that she doesn't. She sounds like she's crying her heart out. How could Jason have done this to her? And by *text*? That is so cowardly!

"Oh, Jess, I'm so, so, so sorry."

"I made him a *bracelet*!" she sobs. "I thought he was my *boyfriend*!"

"He doesn't deserve you," I tell her loyally. Should I ask her what Jason said, or typed? I decide not to. If Jess wants me to know what the fateful text was, she'll tell me.

"That's awful, Jess," I say. "What can I do to help?"

There's a pause as my best friend sniffles. "Nothing," she says, in the saddest voice I've ever heard.

There's a light skim of frost on the grass the next morning when I meet Jess at our usual corner. She looks like a train wreck. Her whole face is puffy, and her eyes have such red rims she must have been crying all night.

"I am furious at him!" I say, giving Jess a big hug.

"Look at my eyes," she wails. "I can't go to school like this!"

"You look fine," I say. We both know it's not true, but this is hardly the time to be brutally honest.

"I begged Mom to let me stay home, but she wouldn't," she sniffs. "Why are parents so harsh?"

"It's a good thing you didn't," I tell her. "You can't miss the stop tech."

"I don't even care," says Jess, and I gulp. This is huge. Jess is the only person I know who cares about theatre as much as I do. This Jason thing has thrown her completely off base.

I take her hand, squeezing it sympathetically. "We've got to get going," I tell her gently. "We're going to be late for homeroom."

Jess nods, and we start up the hill hand in hand, just like when we were little. I'm trying to figure out what my best friend needs most from me, but this is all new territory. Should I tell her again how wrong Jason is, or will that just reopen the floodgates? I better just play this by ear.

"I love you, Jess," I finally tell her, and she sniffles, "Thanks. Love you, too."

We walk all the way up Underhill Avenue without saying another word. Jess's breathing is getting more even, and she isn't clenching my hand as hard, so it seems like she's getting calmer. I hope so.

Just before we turn into the middle school driveway, she stops, reaches into her pocket, and puts on a pair of sunglasses. "Just until we get inside," she says. "Do I look insane?"

"Not at all," I assure her, though a Mad Hatter top hat and blue Ray-Bans is not quite your typical middle school look. Whatever she needs to get through this, I figure. But as soon as we get to the flagpole, we run smack into Ethan

Horowitz, coming down the stairs of his school bus with an ear-to-ear grin.

"Hey, check it out, it's this year's winner of the Johnny Depp look-alike contest," he smirks. "Groovy shades, man."

"Ethan, back off!" I say sharply.

"Oh, whoa, it's the fashion police," he says, putting his hands up. "Jessica Munson, you're under arrest."

And then the worst possible thing happens. Jess bursts into tears.

"Go away," she sobs. "Leave me alone."

The change that comes over Ethan's face is instantaneous. "Oh my god, I'm so sorry," he says. "I didn't mean . . . Jess? I'm an idiot."

"It's okay," Jess sniffles. "It's not your fault. It's just me."

Ethan looks at me, wondering what he should do. And then he surprises us both. He opens his arms to give Jess a shy, awkward hug. "Whatever it is, it's all right," he says. "Okay, Jess? It's cool."

That *is* pretty cool. Good for Ethan!

• • •

Amelia and I have first-period gym, and I tell her how Jason dumped Jess. "No way!" she exclaims. "What a *jerk*!"

"No kidding," I say, still fuming on Jess's behalf.

"She should kick his butt," says Amelia, bending down to tie her sneaker.

"Hard," I agree. "How did your dress rehearsal for *Nutcracker* go last night?"

"All right, I guess," says Amelia. "I can't wait till it's over."

"Aren't you excited?" I ask her, even as I feel a pang of nervousness about my own role in it. "You open *tonight*!"

"Don't remind me," she says gloomily. "You've got your tickets, right?"

I nod. "I can't wait. Fay is bringing the twins, but I got permission to go with Sara and" — we look at each other — "Jess."

"Ouch," says Amelia. "She's going to be *totally* not in the mood for the whole handsome prince thing."

"Well, it's a distraction, right? Better than staying at home," I say.

"Hey," says Amelia, "*I'd* rather stay home."

"You don't count," I say as we head for the door to the gym. Just before we go through it, Amelia turns toward me.

"Oh. When I give you the signal, ask Coach Ridley for a bathroom pass."

"Okay," I say. "Why?"

"You'll see," says Amelia. "I'll tug on my ear."

We're playing volleyball, a sport I'm actually *not* horrible at, so the time passes fast. Ten minutes before the end of class, I notice Amelia is tugging her ear in a weird and insistent way. Duh! It's the signal.

Our team's on the bench, so her timing is perfect. "Coach Ridley?" I say, raising my hand. "Can I go to the bathroom?"

She nods, and I head for the lockers. Less than a half minute later, Amelia meets me. "So what's the big secret?" I ask her.

She opens her locker and takes out a bag. "Follow me," she says, and we go to the row of sinks. There's a long strip of mirror above them. Amelia reaches into her bag and starts taking out makeup: lipstick, eyebrow pencils, a tin of clown white.

"What is this?" I gasp.

"Your doll face," she says. "The makeup woman taught me last night. Just do the same thing that I do."

She digs her fingertips into the clown white. "I hate how this feels," she says. "It's like grease."

"It's called greasepaint," I tell her. "It *is* grease."

We cover our faces with white, including our eyebrows and lips. Amelia draws on a thin black arch, high above where her natural eyebrow would be, and I follow suit. Then she draws on eyeliner, adding big, doll-like lashes.

"That looks so fake," I say.

"It's supposed to look fake," she says. "You're a *doll*."

She draws a high circle of rouge on each cheek. "Okay, this is the weird part. You ready?"

I nod. Amelia picks up the lipstick, a vivid bright red, and makes two little dots on the bottom and top of her whited-out lips.

"Really?" I say. "That small?"

"Uh-huh. You'll see how it works with the wig."

I draw on my mini lips. Even without the wig, the effect is strikingly doll-like. And ignoring the fact that my hair is dark brown and Amelia's is blond, we look very much alike. "That's pretty cool," I say. "Look at us."

We look at ourselves side by side in the mirror, and then hear a voice right behind us. "Ladies?"

Startled, we both whip around to see Coach Ridley, standing just inside the door with a volleyball in one hand and a whistle around her neck. She stares at our makeup and shakes her head slowly. "You know what? I don't want to hear it," she says. "Wash your faces this second."

We do.

Chapter Seven

The last tech rehearsal drags on for hours. While the tech crew figures out the lighting, music, and sound cues, we actors sit around in the hall running lines. I notice that Marisol and Riley are sitting together as usual, but Ethan is off to one side, and keeps glancing at Jess like he's worried about her.

He has reason to worry: Jess really isn't herself. She sits staring down at the floor with her arms wrapped around her knees. I try to distract her by offering to help her run lines, but she snaps, "I *know* my lines. I just don't feel *funny*. At all."

"Well, let's run them anyway," I urge her. "Ms. Wyant said we should practice." I read the first couple of cues, and

Jess drawls out her lines in a monotone. I cue her again, and she looks me right in the eye.

"I can't believe I made him that bracelet," she says.

"It was beautiful, too," I say.

"Yeah. It was."

At last we get to the end of Act Two, and most of the cast goes onstage for the final production number. Because I'm not in that, I sit in the back of the auditorium and try to imagine that I'm in the audience. Some of the cast are in costumes, some in their street clothes plus crowns. There might be a few production glitches to solve, but the bottom line is everyone sounds pretty good. Even Kayleigh.

After the rehearsal, I walk home with Jess. It's already dark — the thing I hate most about this time of year — and a wind has come up, so I wrap my scarf tighter around my neck. The last thing I need at this point is a cold!

When we get to the corner, Jess says abruptly, "Well, bye," and starts toward her house. I follow her. "Where are you going?" she asks, whirling to face me.

"I'm invited to dinner at your house. We're going

to Amelia's opening night, remember? Your mom's getting pizzas?"

"You're kidding," says Jess.

"Did you really forget?" I'm actually concerned now.

"I can't go," says Jess. "I don't want to see a ballet. I just want to crawl into my bed and stay there."

"That's not going to help and you know it," I say. "Besides, your mom is driving. And we promised Amelia."

Jess looks at me for a long moment. "You're right," she says finally. "I have to get over this. Just give me a minute, okay? There's something that I've got to do."

I nod, wondering what it could be. Jess walks to the curb and stands next to a sewer grate. She reaches into her pocket, takes out the blue-and-tan-and-maroon friendship bracelet, and drops it into the sewer.

"GOOD RIDDANCE!" she screams at the top of her lungs. Then she turns to me, smiling. "Much better. Let's go eat pizza."

Sara joins us for dinner and so does Dash, who steals pepperoni off everyone's slices. Mrs. Munson's upstairs in her room, changing out of her nursing scrubs. She comes back downstairs in corduroy slacks and a forest green sweater that brings out the red in her rusty brown hair. It's easy to see where Jess and Dash got their coloring.

"Everyone ready?" she asks, and we nod. She picks up the two empty pizza boxes and tosses them into the trash with the paper plates. "My kind of cleanup," she says with deep satisfaction. I know how she feels.

Dash folds his arms, looking pouty. "Do I *have* to go?" he says with a whine that gives Brynna a run for her money.

"Have I already answered that question?" his mother asks patiently.

"Whyyyy?" moans Dash.

"Because you're not old enough to stay home by yourself." Mrs. Munson picks up a cone of chrysanthemums with a yellow bow.

"But I could go over to Noah's. He said so."

"His mother did not," Mrs. Munson says. "And besides, it'll do you good to watch something that's not on a screen."

"And where nothing explodes," Jess smirks. "Except you, from too much pepperoni." I think she's bounced back.

• • •

The Nutcracker is being performed at the Rosendale Concert Hall, a restored vaudeville theatre that's only a few miles away — a good thing, because Mrs. Munson, as usual, is running late. On the marquee, in bright, glowing letters, are the words:

FLEET FEET BALLET SCHOOL
presents
THE NUTCRACKER

It gives me a thrill to scurry under those lights — I'm sort of a part of the cast, after all — and follow Mrs. Munson to the ticket taker. The interior is an odd mix of freshly repainted walls and faded original carpets. "Cool!" Jess breathes, looking up at the old chandeliers. "They're like something from *Phantom*!"

Amelia has gotten us excellent seats — on the center aisle, about ten rows back. I spot Fay and the twins in the second row, way off to one side. I hope they'll be able to see the whole set from that angle, but even if not, the girls will enjoy being so close. As I sit between Sara and Jess, the lights start to fade. Dash slumps down in the aisle seat, already convinced that he'd rather be anyplace else on the planet.

The music is recorded, and though I miss hearing the pit orchestra tune up, the magic begins with the very first notes. The blue velvet curtain rolls up, revealing a scrim with a painting of an elegant town house. As we watch, the lights change to make it transparent, and we see a grand parlor decorated for Christmas, with a large, lavish tree. Servants are preparing for a party as the master and mistress instruct them on finishing touches. A boy in a sailor suit enters, followed by a girl in an old-fashioned party dress. Sara elbows my ribs, whispering, "It's Zoe!"

She's right. It's Amelia's big sister, who I've never seen looking so graceful and gorgeous. She moves like a star. I can see why they cast her as Clara.

Party guests start to arrive, and it's fun to recognize most of their costumes. Thanks to Cinderella Cleaners, I know this show inside out — literally. A mysterious figure in a green velvet opera cape sweeps through the door. He keeps his face covered, but I'd know that cape anywhere.

It belongs to the toy maker, Drosselmeyer. After circling the room in a sinister crouch, he throws back the cape and reveals himself, with a bald head and an eye patch.

"It's *that guy*!" whispers Jess, and indeed, it is Mikhail Zaloom, Fleet Feet's pompous ballet master.

Drosselmeyer turns back to the door and gestures to two of the servants to bring in two oversize gift boxes. I hold my breath and sit forward in my seat, knowing the first box he opens is going to contain . . .

A mechanical doll. In a dress I know well.

"Wow!" Sara says, loud enough that someone turns to shush her.

"Is that *her*?" whispers Jess, and I nod.

In her black wig and white face paint, Amelia is unrecognizable, and she does her dance perfectly. I can feel my body making the same moves in my seat, my wrists stiffening into right angles and neck dropping off to one side as the doll's windup mechanism slows down, leaving her frozen in place. Drosselmeyer throws open the second box, revealing a boy in a jumping jack costume. Must be Eli the nerd.

The rest of the first scene swims by in a blur as I nervously ponder how I'm going to pull this off. Then, onstage, the grandfather clock starts to chime.

One . . . two . . . three . . .

I hear Dash exclaim, "Whoa!" as the Christmas tree behind sleeping Zoe gets bigger and bigger. How do they *do* that?

. . . eleven . . . twelve.

At the stroke of midnight, the first mice appear. They're played by the school's youngest students, and they're kind of funny, with big face masks and gloved hands held up like small paws. But they're followed by mice who can really dance, and then, with a huge roll of music, the Mouse King sweeps onto the stage. Except . . . she's a Mouse *Queen*!

Nontraditional casting, for sure, but she's a sensational dancer. This must be the professional ballerina Amelia calls Diva Central, the Russian one married to . . .

OMG! There he is: Nikolai Chodoff, the Nutcracker Prince. He grand jetés onto the stage with the same crackling energy as Baryshnikov, and he looks just as good in his uniform jacket and tights. No wonder Zoe has a crush on him!

Sara and Jess both sit forward at once. It was fun watching the students perform, but these two are total professionals, and their battle dance is electrifying. Even Dash seems impressed, though that might be because an army of toy soldiers with swords has just joined the battle.

The Nutcracker Prince is outnumbered, and the Mouse Queen seems certain to win. But then comes my favorite moment: Clara picks up one of her slippers and hurls it at the giant mouse's head. The Queen keels over. The mice lift her and carry her offstage, leaving Clara alone with her Prince.

The lights change again, and snow starts falling, transforming the room into a magical snow-covered meadow, and Clara's bed into a sleigh. As the last chords of Act One play, she and her prince are whisked off to the Land of Sweets.

We clap till our palms hurt. "That was terrific!" says Jess, blinking happily.

"How cute is that Nikolai Chodoff guy?" Sara says. "He's a *hunk*!"

Dash points a finger down his throat, pretending to gag, and Jess gives him a swat. "Don't hit your brother, Jess," says Mrs. Munson. "Well, wasn't that fun!"

"The sword part was okay," Dash says. "The rest of it stunk. Can I get some candy?"

We go to the lobby and buy three kinds of chocolates. As we walk away, I see Ashley and Brynna standing next to the water fountain while Fay waits in line for the ladies' room. "How do you like it?" I ask them.

"It was *great*!" Ashley beams, and Brynna nods so enthusiastically that I impulsively give them my caramel chocolates.

"Hey, thanks!" Brynna says, and Ashley echoes, "Yeah, thanks!"

"Sure," I nod, heading outside with my friends. That actually felt kind of . . . good. Maybe Dad had a point with this ladies' night out.

Sara, Jess, and I huddle under the marquee, enjoying the nip of fresh air as we stuff our faces with chocolate and gossip about the show.

"So who's the Nutcracker hunk?" Jess asks.

"He's one of the teachers at Fleet Feet," says Sara. "He was a professional dancer, but he had a really bad injury."

"Really?" says Jess. "Because he wasn't moving like *anything* hurt him."

"I guess it's like athletes," says Sara. "They learn how to live with it. But his wife is the real pro, Amelia told me. She danced at the Bolshoi Ballet."

"And never lets anybody forget it," I add, reaching for one of the chocolate mints.

"The Mouse Queen?" asks Jess, and Sara nods.

"Zaloom wanted her to be Clara, but she took a cameo part so she wouldn't have to waste time rehearsing with *students*. She gives them all attitude," Sara says.

"Sounds like Kayleigh in toe shoes," says Jess. "What's her name?"

"I forget. Something Russian," says Sara.

"Amelia calls her Diva Central," I say. "But her real name must be in the program." Jess is the only one who brought her program outside. But as soon as she starts flipping through it, an usher walks by ringing chimes.

We rush back to our seats for Act Two, which takes place in the Land of Sweets. Again, I take special pride in seeing the costumes we cleaned and repaired: the Turk in his turban, the Chinese ribbon dancers, the Spanish duet. And then there's *another* duet, this one danced by Amelia and Eli. As I watch them doing the intricate movements, my jaw drops, and Jess nudges me in the ribs. "Are you swan-faking *this* dance on Saturday, too?"

"No way!" I say, turning to Sara. "Whatever you do, make *sure* that Amelia gets back here before intermission!"

"No kidding," says Sara as we watch Amelia. Zoe might be the family star, but if Amelia had chosen ballet over soccer, she'd probably be just as good. I'm really impressed.

The next dance is a comic one — Mother Ginger comes out in her giant hoopskirt, fanning her face with a folding lace fan. Something about her looks familiar.

"Is it that Zaloom guy again?" Jess whispers, and I realize that it's him, in a wig. But that isn't the only surprise: Out of Mother Ginger's skirt comes a whole group of gingerbread children, danced by the same beginning students who played the young mice. They're adorable.

Last but not least is the Dance of the Sugar Plum Fairy,

who is a long-legged Brazilian beauty in toe shoes. She must be another professional dancer, because her every move makes me gasp. It's a pleasure to watch her dance with Nikolai Chodoff.

Is this what it feels like to swoon? I find myself thinking of Will and that moment we shared on the piano bench. It makes me blush, and I'm grateful it's dark.

Finally, the curtain comes down on Clara, curling up with her wooden toy nutcracker. We clap and clap, and then clap some more. I thought the curtain calls for Broadway musicals went on for a long time, but they're nothing like this. Every group of dancers comes out individually, bowing and curtsying, working their way up from gingerbread children and party guests to the featured performers, and finally the stars.

We clap extra hard for Amelia, and Sara chants her name.

I would have thought Zoe would get the last bow — she's playing the lead, after all — but that's not how they do it in ballet world: She's just a student. She does get a solo curtain call, and her mother comes out from the wings and gives her an armload of roses. Then Zoe steps off to one side, and Nikolai Chodoff comes out for his bow, looking handsome and flushed.

The audience jumps to its feet for a standing ovation. Is it my imagination, or is Jess clapping louder than anyone else? Take *that*, Jason Geissinger, text dumper!

The next solo bow is the Sugar Plum Fairy, who drops a deep, graceful curtsy. Again, she's presented with roses.

That has to be it, I think, but no, there's one more. Out comes the Mouse Queen, who drops twice as low as the Sugar Plum Fairy, giving her curtsy a dying swan flutter.

Talk about hamming it up! And her part wasn't even that big — it must be that Bolshoi Ballet training that gave her top billing.

But wait! Diva Central did *not* get top billing. There's one ham even bigger than she is, and here he comes now: Mikhail Zaloom, in his Drosselmeyer cape. The ovation goes on and on. At long last, he holds up his hand, and the audience settles and starts sitting down.

Jess and I look at each other with a horrified realization: He's going to make one of his *speeches*!

"Ladies and gentlemen, lovers of dance," he begins. "I am *humbled. . . .*"

• • •

Dash flatly refuses to join us backstage, so Mrs. Munson relents and takes him to the car, handing Jess the chrysanthemums for Amelia. This suits me just fine; I need a backstage tour so I'll know the lay of the land when I get there on Saturday.

The day after tomorrow, I think, gulping.

Amelia's told us where to look for her, warning, "Don't go anywhere near the stars' dressing rooms, *ever*." Sounds like good advice.

The ballet students in the cast cluster inside a greenroom that reminds me of our middle school music room. Amelia's mother hovers over the group like a big hummingbird. Proud parents are hugging their daughters and sons and snapping their photos with cell phones and digital cameras.

Finally, we spot Amelia, who's already scrubbing the paint off her face with a towel. "One down, four to go," she says.

"Three and a half," I correct her.

"That's right," grins Amelia. "So what did you think?"

"You rocked!" says Jess, handing her the chrysanthemums.

"Awesome!" says Sara.

"You dance *really* well," I tell her, "and if you don't get back by that Act Two duet, I'll break both your legs."

"No worries," says Amelia. "Come on, let me give you a tour."

She leads us around the backstage area. "There's the costume room, see? But don't worry, I'm stashing my costume — *our* costume — somewhere else." Amelia leads us around the corner, opens a door at the end of the hall, and goes under a stairwell to open a second door. She motions us closer.

"See this?" says Amelia. "It's a one-seater bathroom, lockable door. The cast has their own bathrooms, next to the dressing rooms. Nobody knows about this one. I'm coming in early on Saturday, so I'll sign in and pick up my costume. And I'll hang it up on that hook with my makeup kit, wig, and Mom's ballet slippers. Got it?"

I nod. "And where am I meeting you afterward?"

"Here. Come straight to this bathroom as soon as you're done with your dance in Act One. I'll be back before intermission, and we'll have plenty of time to trade clothes. The door to the outside is just down that hallway." She points.

I have to admit, it does sound pretty foolproof. As long as she's right about plenty of time, it should work out just fine. But I've got one more question.

"How do I get from here to the stage?"

"Oh, *details*," Amelia scoffs. "Good one. I'll show you."

She leads all three of us back past the greenroom and into the wings. But the stage isn't empty. A photographer's firing off shots of Nikolai Chodoff, flanked by the Sugar Plum Fairy and the Mouse Queen, both holding their bouquets of roses.

The photographer says, "Just one more."

An accented voice echoes from inside the oversize mouse mask. "No more! Enough more! I am dyink in here!"

She pulls off the Mouse Queen's crowned head, shaking out her sweaty ponytail, and I get the shock of my life.

Diva Central is *Lara Nekrasova*!

Chapter Eight

I have never come so close to fainting. Of all the Russian girls in New Jersey, it had to be *Lara*? How can she be married to the gorgeous Nikolai Chodoff?

But I don't have time to think about that. She's striding our way, and I *can't* let her see me! Thinking fast, I bury my face in Amelia's shoulder and give her a hug, as if I just ran into her this very minute. "Congratulations," I say, making sure to muffle my voice. "You were *so great*!"

Amelia starts to say, "What are you —" but I cut her off, hissing, "Go with it!" Speaking louder, I bubble, "You want me to carry your flowers?"

"Um, sure," says Amelia, and hands me the paper cone. I hold it in front of my face as the now-headless Mouse

Queen strides past, closely followed by Nikolai Chodoff, who's trying to soothe her in Russian.

"Let's get out of here. Fast!" I hiss to my friends, and we scurry back into the wings. I'm terrified that we'll cross paths with Lara, but we can't make it to the door without going back down the same hall.

"What's going on?" Jess says in a stage whisper.

Before I can explain, we run into a bottleneck. Every parent with a camera wants a photo of the Nutcracker Prince, and Nikolai Chodoff obliges, even as Lara stalks off to her dressing room, slamming the door.

That's better, I think. But a diva's a diva, and she might come slamming back out here to yell at her husband. "Come on," I say anxiously, eyeing the door with the star on it. "Let's go!" We press through the crowd, which is no easy matter, but as soon as we get to the costume shop, my heart stops.

Standing at the costume rack, putting a toy soldier's coat on a hanger, is *Lara*!

Again.

Only this time Lara is wearing her street clothes, her hair pulled up into a neat bun with a pencil stuck through it.

It's completely impossible. Ten seconds ago, I saw

her fully dressed in a mouse costume, slamming into a dressing room.

Are there *two* of her? It's my personal nightmare!

As I stand staring through the open door, I hear someone swish angrily past. It's Mouse Queen Lara, throwing her head mask at pencil-bun Lara and snapping out some kind of insult in Russian. Pencil-bun Lara cringes and seems to apologize.

I've seen enough. This is weirder than Christmas trees growing and nutcrackers turning to princes! I turn on my heel and stomp back toward the stairwell, with Amelia, Sara, and Jess trailing after me.

"What's going on?" Jess demands.

"It's Lara Nekrasova!"

"Who is?" asks Jess.

"I don't know! There's two of her!" I wail.

Amelia starts laughing.

"It's not funny," I tell her. "I'm going insane!"

"They're *twins*," says Amelia.

I look at her. "Twins?"

Amelia nods. "Yulia's the Mouse Queen, and her sister Lara is helping backstage with the costumes."

No wonder she brought all the *Nutcracker* costumes to Cinderella Cleaners! And twins, duh. You'd think with twin stepsisters, I would have thought of that, but seeing Lara at all, much less *twice*, freaked me out.

But I still can't believe my bad luck. I was worried enough about Amelia's mother or Zoe recognizing me in the doll costume, but now I'll be backstage with someone who has it in for me and would *love* to get me into more trouble with Dad.

I turn to Amelia. "I'm sorry. I can't go through with this."

Amelia's face falls. "What? I'm *counting* on you!"

"You don't understand. Lara is my worst enemy at the cleaners. She'd love to see me lose my job." My voice sounds as desperate as I feel.

"Diana, she won't ever *see* you. You don't have to go into the costume shop; I'm going to stash the dress in the bathroom for you." Amelia sounds really stressed out. "And you *promised*."

"I know," I tell her. "But —"

"No buts," says Amelia. "You promised you'd help, and there's nobody else. I have to get into this soccer camp."

"Please?" Sara says. "We're both counting on you."

Talk about pressure! I look at Jess, already knowing what she's going to say. "Amelia snuck you into the masquerade ball," Jess reminds me. "You owe her one. Anyway, that's what friends do."

That *is* what friends do, and I know it. I can't break my promise.

"I'll be there," I tell Amelia. She breaks into a grin and says, "Cool."

It *is* cool. So why do I feel so awful?

I can't get to sleep. It's way after bedtime, and I'm staring up at my *Playbill*-covered ceiling and thinking about all the promises I've made and broken this year — especially the ones to my dad about not wearing customers' clothes. It's not just that I'm scared I'll be busted by Lara backstage, it's the whole thing I'm doing. I know in my gut that it just isn't right. Once again, I'm putting on a garment that was dry-cleaned by Cinderella Cleaners, and pretending to be someone else. Even if I'm not forced to out-and-out lie — after all, nobody's likely to ask me, "Are you going to dress up as Amelia at Saturday's *Nutcracker* matinee?" — my actions certainly aren't what I would call honest. I do owe my friend a big favor, but I wish it didn't involve so much sneaking around.

Especially because I am really, truly, deep-down excited and, let's face it, *scared* about singing my solo on Saturday night. If I didn't have this huge hurdle to cross before opening night, I could just concentrate on *The Snow Queen* and being at my very best. But I can't. I've got Mount Nutcracker to climb.

Or fall off with a thud.

My window is open a crack, and a gust of cool wind stirs the air in my room, bringing a whiff of pine. I look over at my little mini tree, and it looks just as lonely as I feel tonight. It's not even a tree, just a bundle of branches shoved into a big vase and decorated with dangle earrings and sparkly hair clips. The angel on top is one of my childhood dolls, and right below her white lace skirt I've circled the tips of the branches with my mother's pearls. It seemed like a sweet private tribute when I hung them up there, but seeing them just makes me sad. If my life were a musical, this would be my ballad moment.

I roll over and close my eyes, hoping to dream about

dancing snowflakes and sugar plum fairies . . . and who knows, maybe even a prince in a rock-and-roll T-shirt.

I don't see Will until Friday's lunch, when the whole *Snow Queen* gang, plus Amelia and Sara, meets at our usual table. Nobody seems to have much of an appetite except Riley, who's famous for eating whatever, whenever; we call him the Iron Stomach. Even the usually boisterous Ethan seems worried. Today Jess is neither as glum as she was yesterday morning nor as punchy as she got last night. She's just quiet. Which isn't like Jessica Munson at all.

Quiet *is* like Will Carson. He sits down in the chair next to mine, but he doesn't say much except "Hey." To be fair, I don't either.

Our dress rehearsal isn't till seven o'clock — same time as the show — so we'll all have this afternoon free to get even more nervous. Luckily, I have something to distract me: the Secret Santa exchange at the cleaners today.

I ride on my usual bus after school but get off a few stops before Sam's Diner. It's a short walk past a strip of mini-mall stores, and I have a quest. I pass Dunkin' Donuts and

Bodacious Bagels and walk into my favorite shop in the area, Kim's Golden Treasures.

Mr. Kim is a kindly Korean man who greets every customer as if there was nobody he'd rather see on the planet. When I was a little girl, he used to fold me origami cranes while I browsed every shelf in his store, full of lucky cat statues, embroidered pajamas, and wonderfully strange candies. He and my grandpapa were buddies when Papa was running the cleaners, and often ate lunch together.

"Miss Diana!" he greets me. "So happy to see you!"

"Thanks, Mr. Kim," I beam.

"So tall and grown-up now," Mr. Kim says. "How can I help you?"

"I'm looking for chopsticks," I tell him. "A really nice pair."

Mr. Kim smiles. "You have come to right place." He sets down his Korean newspaper and leads me back to the grocery section. Next to the packets of rice noodles and jars of fish sauce and kimchee is a virtual banquet of chopsticks. There are blocks of plain wooden ones, lacquer ones like the chopsticks that Gracie was wearing, carved rosewood inlaid with mother-of-pearl. I never knew there were so many different styles of chopsticks! There's even a pink pair with a Hello Kitty design.

Somehow I don't think that's the right choice for my Secret Santa gift. I look over at Mr. Kim. "Do you know Mr. Li Chen, from the cleaners?" I ask him.

"Of course! He is here all the time," he says. "Wonderful man. Very smart."

"I'm picking out a small gift for him," I explain. "I know he collects fancy chopsticks. Can you tell me what he might not have yet?"

Mr. Kim looks over the chopstick bins, frowning. Then he breaks into a smile. "I have chopsticks that nobody has yet," he says. "Just arrived." He walks through a beaded curtain that leads to a storage room. I can hear him inside, moving boxes around.

As I'm waiting, I browse down the clothing aisle, looking at kimonos and brocade slippers. Suddenly I spot a T-shirt I know Will would love. It's a samurai warrior, drawn in traditional costume and style, except for one detail: Instead of a sword, he's holding a bright red electric guitar.

There's only one shirt with this pattern, and it's a size medium. Perfect! I wonder how much it costs. And I wonder if I have the nerve to give Will a cool gift. If he doesn't give me something, too, will he be embarrassed? Will I?

"Look at these!" Mr. Kim's voice startles me, and I turn. He brings over a small box of hand-painted chopsticks with carvings on top. No two pairs are alike, and I know I've found the perfect present. It's only a matter of which ones to pick.

After studying all of the options, I narrow it down to a maroon pair with delicate cherry blossoms and a royal blue pair with carved koi fish.

"Which do you think?" I ask Mr. Kim, and without hesitation he points to the koi.

"Great. I'll take them," I say.

"Is there anything else?" Mr. Kim asks, and I look at the samurai T-shirt.

"Yes. This," I say, picking it up.

So I *do* have the nerve!

Cat is already at work when I get to the cleaners with my Secret Santa gift, beautifully wrapped by Mr. Kim. "Hello, stranger!" she greets me. "Is the stage, screen, and ballet star coming to visit the little people?"

"She's coming to kick your sarcastic butt," I grin. "It's Secret Santa day."

"Duh," says Cat. "Mine is already down deep in the Santa sack."

"Which is?"

"Hanging on your father's door," says Cat. "Really, you'd think you had never been here in your life."

"I've been here *all* my life," I say. "Just not for the holiday party." I glance over my shoulder at Mr. Li Chen, silently working his steam presser. The wrapped chopsticks are safely disguised in a neutral brown bag, so that no one will know who his Santa is. Not till it's time.

And I wonder again who *my* Secret Santa is. Could it be Chris, bopping to the Black Eyed Peas as he mops up a spill? Loretta or Sadie? What would happen if *Dad* drew my name?

Anybody but Lara, I say to myself as I head to the customer counter. I'm positive she didn't see me last night, but I still can't help worrying. What if she catches me backstage tomorrow? I will be so dead.

I push open the swinging doors and step into Customer Service. Sure enough, Lara looks up from the cash register and narrows her eyes at me. I smile and say hi and she looks away. *All right*, I think, *be that way.*

But as I go to Dad's office, I have a sudden memory of a different Lara: the one who was cringing in front of her sister's bad temper. In our bullying prevention unit in health class, we learned that most people who bully have been bullied themselves and try to save face by picking on somebody else. I don't know why Lara chose me as her target, but knowing that her diva twin bosses her around makes me feel a little bit sorry for her.

But only a little.

The red Santa sack on the back of Dad's door is bulging with packages, large and small. I drop mine inside and duck through the door to say hi to Dad.

"Hello, honey," he says, rising to give me a bear hug. "Good to see you back at Cinderella. We've missed you this week."

"Me, too," I tell him, and that is the truth. "Is there anything I can help out with?"

Dad glances up at the clock. It's almost five; I spent more time than I realized browsing at Mr. Kim's Golden Treasures and walking the rest of the way. "Secret Santa begins at five-thirty. I bet Nelson could use a spare elf."

"You bet!" I say, grinning from ear to ear. Something tells me that I'm going to love this tradition.

I walk out past the counter, where Miss MacInerny greets me with a sharp "Diana, where is your smock?"

"I'm not working today," I remind her, pushing open the door to the Tailoring section. The area is completely transformed. The cutting table, always cluttered with fabric scraps and pins, is covered with jolly red fabric. Sadie and Loretta, both wearing green elf caps, are setting out platters of cut veggies and big bowls of chips. Nelson stands on Chris's stepladder, festooning the walls with swags of velveteen ribbon.

"Welcome to Santa's Workshop," he says. "*Now* it's a party."

For the next twenty minutes I scurry around, fetching dips from the mini-fridge and rinsing off grapes in the ladies' room sink. Chris lugs in a tub full of sodas and ice.

At exactly five-thirty, Miss MacInerny locks the front door behind the last customer and flips over the OPEN sign to read CLOSED.

The whole staff gathers around the red table in Tailoring, and suddenly I hear a voice I'd know anywhere, booming a loud "Ho, ho, ho!" Dad comes through the door wearing a fake beard and Santa suit, with the belt strapped around a fake belly. He's lugging the sack of presents over one shoulder.

Is it any wonder I like to dress up and do theatre? It's in my blood!

Everyone claps, and Dad sets down the sack on a card table. "Cinderella Cleaners has had a wonderful year," he begins. "It's been tough at times, but for me, the great gift has been working with all of you. And now it's time to exchange some little gifts. Diana, will you be the elf?"

Lara shoots me an envious look as Sadie takes off her green elf hat and places it onto my head. "Cutest elf in New Jersey," she says.

What does the elf do? I wonder. Dad answers before I can ask. "Pass out one gift at a time," he says. "So we can see them get opened."

The very first gift goes to Cat. It's an orange suede headband, exactly her style. "Too cool!" she says, putting it right on her head. "Thank you, Secret Santa!"

I reach into the gift sack again and again, as employees unwrap gifts that are unexpectedly thoughtful or laugh-out-loud funny. The largest package is for Dad. Somebody's wrapped up a fake mounted-wall fish that sings "Don't Worry, Be Happy" when you press a button. Dad exclaims cheerfully, "*Just* what I always wanted!"

There are only a few gifts left. Sadie gets lavender-scented pot holders; Loretta, perfume. I hand Mr. Chen his package and hold my breath as he unwraps it. When he sees the chopsticks with koi fish, his face breaks into a wide smile. "Magnificent!" he says in perfect, unaccented English. "Somebody knows just what I like."

This makes me feel so good I almost "out" myself by blurting, "Your granddaughter Gracie told me!" Luckily, I catch myself just in time.

My own gift is the last in the bag. It's small, neatly wrapped, and not heavy at all. What can be in it? I open the box, peel back the pink tissue paper, and gasp. Someone has bought me five pairs of different patterned shoelaces for my mix-and-match Converses! "These are *sick*!" I exclaim, and Dad explains, "That's a compliment." Everyone laughs.

"All right," says Dad. "Time for round two. Everyone gets one chance to guess who their Secret Santa was. If you guess right, we put your card into the hat for the grand prize. Let's go in reverse order. Diana, who do you think was your Santa?"

I look around at the circle of faces. It's got to be Nelson or Cat. Someone who knows me really well. But Loretta did give me a certain sly look, and Chris has complimented my mismatched shoelaces style more than once. Come to think of it, everyone here knows me pretty well. "I'm going to guess Cat," I finally say.

She shakes her head, grinning. "Nuh-uh, girlfriend."

Dad intones, "Secret Santa, reveal yourself." And much to my shock, the hand that goes up is none other than . . . Miss MacInerny's.

Joyless? No way!

"Thank you," I splutter. "How did you know?"

Joyless actually *smiles*. "You wear different shoelaces every week, so I figured you must enjoy them."

She's right, of course, but I can't believe that she noticed. Maybe I've been too harsh on her. "Thank you," I say again, still in shock, as Dad continues around the circle. Will Mr. Chen guess that I'm the one who bought his chopsticks? That would be wild!

But he points at his wife, Rose, who laughs and shakes her head.

Nobody else does much better. Most of the guesses are wildly off, and it looks like there's not going to *be* a grand prize. Not until we get back to Cat. She touches her orange headband and says, "Thanks, Mr. Donato."

"How did you know?" Dad asks.

"Chess player," Cat grins. "I know a few things about strategy. Plus, you're the only one left."

"Not fair!" Lara says. "You kept track."

"It's perfectly fair," says Dad. "Fair, square, and *smart*." He hands Cat an envelope. She opens it up and takes out a crisp fifty-dollar bill.

"Whoa!" she says. "Grand prize is right! Thank you so much."

"De nada," says Dad. "Merry Christmas to all!"

That would be enough joy for one day, but it's not over

yet. As everyone's hugging, thanking each other, and picking up snacks, Nelson sidles over to me. "You've got a grand prize, too. Want to see?"

I nod eagerly. "Inside the fitting room," he says. "Check it out."

I pull back the curtain and gasp. Inside is one of the dressmaker mannequins, wearing my Enchantress costume — gown, fur-trimmed cloak, and a gauze-ribbon icicle headdress that's pure Lady Gaga. "Oh, Nelson! It's *fabulous*!"

"Of course," Nelson shrugs. "It's by Nelson Couture."

Chapter Nine

If seeing my costume is fabulous, the dress rehearsal where I get to wear it for the first time is anything but. The theatre cliché is "A bad dress rehearsal means a great opening night." The first part certainly holds true for *The Snow Queen*, when anything that can go wrong does — including my voice cracking on that last high note.

Backstage, Queen Kayleigh torments me ("Such a shame you didn't have enough time to rehearse"), then struts onstage and sings the wrong verse of her big duet with King Riley. "It wasn't *my* fault," she says, storming offstage in a huff. "Those morons on the crew messed up the snow effect. How could I think straight?"

Funny, it didn't seem to throw Riley.

Then Ethan misses an entrance completely, and poor

Marisol's stranded onstage with no scene partner. She tries to improvise, pretending to talk to herself while she paces the royal garden. Meanwhile Jess scrambles back to the music room, hollering, "Ethan! Get out there! You're *on*!" loud enough to be heard in the audience.

Ethan skids onto the stage, yelling "Sorry!" which does not work at all with the opening lines of their romantic scene. Marisol is so rattled she flubs several lines in a row, and even Jess the Jester arriving for comic relief doesn't quite save the day.

Will isn't immune to the dress rehearsal jinx either: His sound cue CD skips a track, so when the sixth-grade peasant lad rings the Styrofoam church bells, the sound that comes out is a cackling hen.

"Got to do something about that bell," wisecracks Jess, "but we need the eggs."

Several people laugh at this, including Miss Bowman, but Kayleigh glares at Jess. By the time we limp into the big finale, complete with an apple tree covered with pink paper blossoms that somehow gets stuck in the wings, the whole cast is ready to cancel the show.

Ms. Wyant manages to stay upbeat as she gives us notes,

but she may be the only person in the whole Drama Club who isn't completely freaked out. "Bad dress, great opening," she repeats. "Seen it happen a million times. You'll pull it out of your hats when you get that performance adrenaline flowing."

But just to be on the safe side, she asks the whole cast to come in at four o'clock tomorrow instead of six, so we can do a quick speed-through.

Great, that's all I need. Now my turnaround time between the *Nutcracker* matinee and *The Snow Queen* will be even tighter. I won't even have enough time to warm up properly. Why in the world did I ever agree to Amelia's scheme?

Well, too late now. I'm in it for better or worse.

Riley raises his hand. "What will we do about dinner?"

"I'll order some sub sandwiches to put in the greenroom," Ms. Wyant says, and Riley beams, "Excellent!"

Only a boy could care about food at a time like this.

As I head for the dressing room, I see Will loping down the aisle with his headphones around his neck.

"Don't try to make me feel better," I tell him. "I totally blew it."

"You and me both," he says. "But your costume's fantastic."

"Thanks. Always nice to be dressed well when you make a fool of yourself."

"You'll ace it tomorrow, you'll see," he says. Then he starts laughing. "But we need the *eggs*?"

When I wake up on Saturday morning, my stomach is tied in more knots than Jess's friendship bracelet. Usually on the morning of opening night, I have a fluttering kind of excitement inside, like butterfly wings. But today I feel sick to my stomach.

I go down the stairs. Dad's pouring coffee into his travel cup. He looks at me. "Someone looks less than well rested," he says. "Are you nervous about your big solo?"

Try my two *big solos.*

"It'll be fine," I say, not too convincingly.

"Want my advice?" says Dad. This isn't a question that parents should ever ask, but instead of intoning some well-meaning speech, he reaches onto the counter and presses the button on his Secret Santa fish — which, by the way, came from Nelson.

"Don't worry, be happy," it starts to sing.

"That's *my* advice," says Dad, kissing the top of my head as he goes out. "I'll see you tonight at the opening."

Only if I'm still alive.

All morning I look at the clock, counting the hours till the end of my life as I know it. Amelia, Sara, and I have already worked out our whole plan, and I'm supposed to be meeting Amelia at the Rosendale Concert Hall at twelve-thirty. But just before noon, Fay throws an unexpected wrench into the works, walking into the kitchen with two pairs of skates.

"Marissa's sick and her mom just canceled skating plans tomorrow. How about taking the girls to the ice rink *today*?" she asks.

"I can't!" I exclaim in a panic. "It's my opening night!"

"Not till seven," says Fay.

"I have an early rehearsal and warm-ups," I protest. "And anyway, what if I broke my" — *I can't say leg, it's bad luck!* — "ankle?"

Fay rolls her eyes. "I can't wait till this nonsense is over."

You and me both, I think as she goes into the living room, where Ashley and Brynna sit watching TV.

"Why can't *you* take us skating?" Ashley demands.

"I can't ice-skate," Fay answers. "My back's acting up."

"You could just sit and watch," Ashley says.

"In the freezing cold ice rink? No, thank you. I'll catch the same cold as Marissa." Fay shudders.

"You could take us to the mall," says Ashley, and Brynna echoes, "Yeah!"

"Not till you clean up your bedroom," says Fay. "Upstairs, march."

The twins grumble, and I look at my phone, relieved. I've only got fifteen minutes to get to the school parking lot, where Sara's aunt Himani is picking me up; her parents are both working the lunch shift at Masala today.

There are already two texts from Amelia:

im here!

and

just got yr costume!!!

I take a deep breath. No avoiding it now. I go up to my bedroom and pack my backpack with my stage makeup, a granola bar, and a scarf, just in case it gets colder tonight. I run quickly through my ballet steps, trying to channel Amelia's performance. Then I look up at my *Playbill*s and take a deep breath. Here goes nothing.

Fay's very surprised to see me heading back downstairs with my backpack and fleece-lined hoodie. "You're leaving *already*?"

"I told you, I have an early rehearsal. I have to go up to the school." Actually, both of these statements are true; they're just not true *together*.

"All afternoon? Will you be back home for dinner?" Fay asks.

I shake my head. "Ms. Wyant is bringing sub sandwiches."

"I'm always the last to know." Fay sounds irritated. "Well. We'll see you there." It's a long way from wishing me luck, but at least she's not putting up roadblocks.

The wind pulls at my coat as I hurry up Underhill Avenue, and I'm glad I'm wearing my hoodie on top of my sweatpants and boring white sneakers — Amelia convinced me that our bottom halves had to match. There's a definite nip in the air, and it's easy to picture snow falling soon. The hillside below our school is a great place for sleds.

I wish I could go sledding right now.

Aunt Himani's car is easy to spot, since it's the color of a ripe tangerine. She's one of my favorites of Sara's big extended family, most of whom work at the restaurant full- or part-time. Aunt Himani always remembers my name and makes a big fuss over me. "Such beautiful brown eyes," she always says. "You could be Indian!"

She drives over to meet me. Sara is in the front passenger seat, already dressed in her soccer uniform. I climb into the back. "Thanks so much for the ride," I tell her.

"Of course, dear," says Himani, checking to see that I've fastened my seat belt before she pulls out into traffic. "We're stopping to pick up Amelia in any case, so it's no trouble. But why are you going so early?"

I hesitate, unsure exactly what Sara and Amelia have told her. "Diana is helping backstage," Sara says, meeting my eyes in the rearview mirror. "She has to be there early to set up the costumes."

I nod. So does Aunt Himani.

"Amelia doesn't come on till the second act," Sara says. "So we'll get back from the tryouts in plenty of time."

"I see," says Aunt Himani. "What part are you dancing, Diana?"

I answer, "A doll," just as Sara says, "Amelia's twin."

We look at each other. "Um, twin dolls," I say quickly. "But I'm in Act One, too."

"And helping with costumes," says Sara.

You can always tell that somebody is covering up when they offer too much information. But Aunt Himani just sighs. "All of you girls are *so* busy."

Well, that part is true, at least!

When we pull up to the Rosendale Concert Hall, Amelia is waiting by the side entrance. She flashes a thumbs-up.

"Thank you so much," I tell Aunt Himani again, giving Sara a pat on the shoulder. "You'll be awesome," I tell her.

"You, too," Sara says. "Break a leotard."

I get out of the car and scurry to the door where Amelia is waiting. She holds up her hand, waves an

"I'll be right back" signal to Sara's aunt, and ducks back inside with me.

"Quick, before anyone sees you," she says, stripping off her A. WILLIAMS soccer team jacket and blue-and-white-striped scarf and hat and layering them onto me, being careful to hide my dark hair completely. She's wearing her soccer team jersey and sweatpants.

"You're going to be great," she says. "And by the way, no one is going to come *near* you — I've been faking a really bad cold since this morning."

"Good thinking," I say.

"I went out to buy cough drops, in case it comes up," Amelia says, grabbing a tote stuffed with her shin guards and cleats. "And you look just like me. It's spooky."

"I hope it goes great," I say. "Text me. And don't be late!"

"Word," says Amelia, and sprints to the car.

I wrap the striped scarf a bit higher to cover my mouth. Now all I have to do is walk into the theatre, remember the way to that single-stall bathroom, put on my costume, and get into makeup before someone sees me.

Especially Lara!

Chapter Ten

Of course I run right into Amelia's mother. "*There* you are, honey!" she says. "I was starting to worry. I shouldn't have let you go out in this chilly wind with a cough."

Cough, I think. *Right*.

I duck my head to one side, lifting my hand as I make coughing noises.

"Oh, dear, you sound worse," says Mrs. Williams. "Let me get you some Emergen-C."

I know what that is. It's a drink, and if I have to unwind this scarf and uncover my mouth, I'll be busted. My heart starts to race. Luckily, Zoe calls out from her dressing room, "Mom? Where did you put my toe pads?"

"They're inside the — I'll be right there!" Mrs. Williams darts off to take care of it. I breathe a sigh of relief and set off for the secret bathroom, carefully turning my head to the side as I slink past the wide-open door of the costume room. I know Lara's in there.

I go into the bathroom and lock the door behind me. My costume is just where Amelia told me she'd leave it, and so are the ballet slippers, black wig, and makeup bag. So far, so good.

I start peeling off layers, hanging Amelia's striped scarf and team jacket on the coat hook. When I'm down to my V-neck and sweatpants, I stretch the black nylon wig cap over my hair. I already look more like a doll.

I lean over the sink, washing my face with soap and water. I apply a thin layer of moisturizer, unscrew the cap of the clown white, and start dabbing it onto my face. Then I rub it in with my fingertips, blending till I have an even layer from forehead to chin, including my lips and eyebrows.

I look at myself in the mirror. With no color at all on my face, I look really eerie, as if I've turned into a ghost. Or a mime.

Remembering Amelia's instructions, I draw on high, arched eyebrows and oversize lashes. Then I paint pink circles of rouge on my cheeks, finishing up with that odd little half mouth. It looks pretty good, considering how jumpy I'm feeling.

Now it's time to get into my costume. I take off my T-shirt and sweatpants and pull on the white tights Amelia has left for me. Next, I zip on that adorable dress, pausing to admire the way Nelson pieced in the gussets so they wouldn't ruin the line of the bodice. As soon as it's on my body, I start to feel that old costume magic transforming me into somebody else, as if I were a real windup doll. The finishing touch is the shiny black wig.

I look at myself in the mirror and have to admit that I don't look a thing like Diana Donato. This helps to settle my nerves. I'm feeling so good that I start to run through the first steps of my dance.

And then somebody knocks on the door.

The panic is instant. One second I'm feeling transformed, the next I'm a wreck. Rasping "Just a minute" with a loud cough, I flush the toilet to buy some more time. My eyes fly around the room. Most of the stuff is Amelia's, and no one would know who the sweatpants and T-shirt belong to, but my backpack with my school ID attached to the front is a dead giveaway. Moving quickly, I stash the

ID card inside the backpack, shove it behind the wastebasket, and open the door up to . . . Nikolai Chodoff!

"Excuse, please, Ameliotchka," he says with a twinkle. He's wearing his street clothes — a striped boatneck sweater and jeans — but there's no mistaking his dancer's grace. "I did not know this vas dressink room now. Are you finish?"

I nod, too starstruck to speak, even if I weren't worried my voice would sound wrong. Grabbing the striped scarf and soccer jacket, I scuttle out into the hall with my heart beating double time.

Now what? It's still half an hour till curtain, and I've just lost my private hideaway. I can't go hang out in the greenroom or wander onstage to practice; I'd surely get caught. My best bet would be finding a new hiding place. I wonder what's up these stairs. Maybe there's some empty office or classroom. Or a janitor's closet — I'm really not fussy. As long as it's empty.

There's only one way to find out.

I don't get very far. The door at the top of the stairway is locked. But the landing is wide enough for me to practice my dance without anyone seeing me. Perfect!

I run through the dance steps three times in a row, till I'm starting to feel pretty confident. Then I have a terrible thought. Does Mikhail Zaloom do the same kind of company pep talk that Ms. Wyant gives us, and if so, what time does it start? We're almost at ten-minute call, and I can't hide forever.

I slip on Amelia's jacket — it makes me feel safer and might help disguise the fact that her shoulders are broader than mine and her arms look much stronger. For extra comfort, and to help spread the myth of my terrible cold, I add her striped scarf. Then I head down the stairs and back into the hall to the greenroom and stage.

The backstage area is much busier now and reminds me a lot of the Drama Club right before a performance. Except the dancers are all doing torturous stretches instead of voice warm-ups. I hope no one expects *me* to stand up against a wall with my leg stretched high over my head!

A few of the dancers greet me as Amelia, and I nod and smile, hoping against hope that the costume and wig will continue to disguise me. Then I see Mikhail Zaloom coming toward me in his Drosselmeyer costume.

He stops in his tracks, flips up his eye patch, and looks me up and down.

Here it comes, I think in terror. *I'm sunk!*

"Good job on the makeup," he finally says. "But do lose that dreadful athletic costume. You're a budding artiste."

I lift a hand to my throat, croaking, "Bad cold."

"Ah," he says, neatly sidestepping me. Whew — it worked!

I've reached the backstage area, and as always, it gives me a thrill to look at a set from the back, where what looks like a solid wall to the audience turns out to be nothing but wood and stretched canvas. There's a very high fly space above me, and dozens of stage lights. I wander out onto the stage, looking up at the magical sight, and nearly trip over a dancer.

Not just any dancer either — she's wearing a royal mouse costume, minus the head, and the face that glares at me looks exactly like Lara Nekrasova's.

"I'm so sorry!" I gasp.

"Clumsy cow," she sneers. "Go play your *futbol*." She turns on her heel and stalks offstage, leaving me speechless.

Wow. Diva Central makes Lara look *nice*.

I head for the opposite wing to examine the oversize gift box I'll have to get into, but the stage manager crosses at a diagonal, saying, "Ten minutes, please. Please clear the stage."

Where am I going to hide for ten minutes? The answer is obvious: inside my box. I look over my shoulder to make sure I'm not in the stage manager's sight lines, then crouch down to climb into the gift box.

It's cozy inside, if a little bit airless. I sit cross-legged, wondering what Amelia and Sara are doing right now. Probably bouncing a soccer ball off their heads.

At last the stage manager calls "Places!" and I hear many feet moving around me. Then I hear the opening chords of the overture. Should I stay in my box or stand in the wings and watch?

I decide it's safer to stay in the box, but I open the front section so I can watch. Being backstage gives me a whole different perspective on what looked so effortless on Thursday night. The dancers come off the stage panting and dripping with sweat. As the party scene goes on, a boy in a jumping jack costume comes over to me. *Eli*, I realize.

"Amelia?" he says in a stage whisper. "How come you're in *my* box?"

Oops.

"Sorry," I whisper back, clambering out. Only then do I realize both of my feet have fallen asleep! I start frantically shaking them, bumping my heels on the floor. Eli stands staring at me like I've lost my mind.

"My feet fell asleep!" I hiss, but his worried expression remains the same.

"Why are you in those clothes?" he asks, and I realize I'm still wearing Amelia's soccer team jacket and scarf! I strip them off quickly, looking for someplace to put them. Limping on my leaden feet, I drop the scarf and jacket on top of a stage weight sandbag in the wings, where they won't be in anyone's way.

A stagehand comes over to help put us into our gift boxes. If I thought it felt airless before, it's thirty times worse with the top closed. It's a good thing I'm not claustrophobic.

Still, it's a shock moments later when I feel the box start to move. The servants must be rolling us onto the stage. *Make it stop!*

This is it, I think. *Try not to blow it.*

I hope my feet work. And I hope I don't faint. Or forget all my steps. Or trip and fall flat on my face. Or —

The box is thrown open, and I'm carried out, standing stiffly as Amelia showed me, even though I'm so nervous I feel like I'm made out of wet noodles. Drosselmeyer swoops over and makes a great show of winding me up. With my heart thumping so hard I think the whole cast must be able to hear it, I lift my arms into position and start. . . . Oh. My. God.

Dancing *ballet*. In front of an audience.

How did I get myself into this mess?

It's a good thing my character's supposed to move stiffly, because I'm almost frozen with fear. I thought I knew what stage fright felt like, but this is out of control. I feel like my whole body's running a fever, and even my greasepaint is sweating.

But Amelia must be a good coach, because even though I feel totally out of my element, somehow I remember the sequence of steps.

Well, most of them anyway. Just as I start to relax a little and think this might not be a total disaster, I turn left when I should have turned right and wind up with my legs twisted into a pretzel again. I don't want to freeze in this knock-kneed position, so as I cock my head to one side for the last "winding down" movement, I jerk my left leg back.

And my left ballet slipper flies off my foot, into the wings!

Zaloom lets out a small gasp. I close my eyes, wincing. I'm in my final pose. I can't turn my head to see where it landed. How could I have made such a stupid mistake? First turning on the wrong foot, and then losing my shoe? Who ever told me I knew how to perform? I'll probably mess up my solo tonight in *The Snow Queen*, too.

Don't even think about that, I tell myself firmly. *One thing at a time.* I still have to get off this stage, find the missing ballet slipper, steer clear of Lara, get out of this costume, and get it back onto Amelia without getting caught.

When Amelia gets back here, that is. And I sure hope it's soon!

Eli has finished his jumping jack dance and we're carried offstage, where there's now a platoon of toy soldiers lining up in one wing and mice gathering in the other, adjusting their head masks.

One of the mice stalks toward me in a fury, and I realize two things that make my blood run cold.

First: It's Diva Central.

Second: She's holding my slipper.

"You kick this at me?" she hisses. "How *dare* you!"

"It was a mistake," I say, my voice shaking.

"*You* are mistake," she says. "Out of my sight!"

"I'm so sorry," I start, but she shakes her head.

"Go!" Feeling about three inches tall, I skulk toward the hall. The only person in the world I want to see is Amelia Williams.

A. WILLIAMS, I think, and remember her soccer jacket and scarf. Looking over one shoulder to make sure Diva Central's not watching, I scuttle around to the spot where I left them . . . but the stage weight is nowhere in sight.

There's only one place it could have gone. Cringing, I crane my neck upward and there it is, hanging thirty feet over the stage, with the jacket and scarf dangling off it!

What should I do? By some miracle, when the stage-hands pulled up the scrim and the counterweight sandbag flew up, the jacket and scarf stayed balanced on top. But will they *stay* there, or fall down onto somebody's head?

I can't believe this is happening! I'm a walking disaster!

The music has gotten dramatic, and I notice a stagehand is pulling on one of the ropes. Little by little, the cloth of the Christmas tree unfolds, so it seems to be growing taller and taller. Someone high up on a ladder dips her hand into a bucket of glitter and soap flakes and lets the mixture sift down through a shaft of light between the windows and the backdrop, and there is that lovely snowfall.

Somehow it seems even more magical, knowing how low-tech the effect really is. And then, as I watch, something else falls down: a blue-and-white Weehawken Middle School scarf!

A ripple of laughter runs through the audience as the scarf gets caught on the Christmas tree, and I hold my breath, praying the soccer jacket won't follow.

Chapter Eleven

The clock starts to chime, and on the stroke of midnight, the first little mice make their entrance. I stand stock-still, praying that none of them will get clobbered by a soccer team jacket tumbling down from above.

The next wave of mice enters, taller and faster, circling around Zoe as Clara. Finally, the Mouse Queen comes leaping onstage. I hate to admit it, but Diva Central is riveting. She's in perfect control of her limbs, cutting a classic ballet silhouette.

How can someone so mean be so talented? It just isn't fair.

And then Nikolai Chodoff grand jetés on as the Nutcracker Prince, sword drawn and legs flashing like scissors. I catch my breath. The ballet students in the cast all know their stuff, but watching these professionals dance from so close is a thrill. I'm totally hooked.

The column of toy soldiers marches on, and the battle scene escalates. The whole stage seems to shake with the trample of feet. It looks like the Mouse Queen is triumphing over the Nutcracker Prince, but then comes my favorite moment, when Zoe as Clara picks up her slipper, draws back her arm, and . . .

And a soccer team jacket falls out of the sky, landing right on the Mouse Queen's head! There's a roar of laughter and applause from the audience.

I stand frozen in panic. She's going to *murder* me!

For the first time in ages, I remember Amelia's instructions: *As soon as you've finished your dance, go back to the bathroom and wait for me there. I'll be back before intermission.* She better be right!

Onstage, the mice are lifting their fallen Queen onto their shoulders. One of the little ones picks up the jacket, getting another huge laugh.

I better get out of here — fast!

Dodging behind the painted backdrop, I dash for the opposite wing and into the hallway that leads past the greenroom to my secret bathroom. As I rush down the hall, I hear the ballet music piped over a dressing room intercom and Act One party guests asking each other, "What just happened? What was that big laugh?"

Almost there, almost there . . .

And then someone steps out of the costume shop.

Lara.

"Vat happened, Amillia?" she asks in a voice like a sword. I can't think of anything else to do. I cover my mouth with both hands as if I'm going to vomit — which I really might, I'm so nervous — and charge past her, rounding the corner, pushing open the door, and beating a path to my hideaway bathroom.

It's *locked*!

I'm definitely going to throw up. Or faint. Can you do both at once?

Not only are all my clothes in that bathroom, my cell phone is inside my backpack. And Amelia is nowhere in sight.

I don't know what to do. This is the worst thing that could possibly happen. I tug hard on the door handle, hoping against hope that this time it will open.

And somebody calls from inside, "Hold your horses, I'm *coming*!"

So much for this being a bathroom that nobody knows about. But I'm so relieved I don't even care. As long as I get to my clothes and my cell phone!

I stand by the wall, my heart pounding like crazy. At long last, the Sugar Plum Fairy sweeps out of the bathroom in full makeup. She looks so stunning I almost bow. I'm afraid she'll be mad that I pounded the door, but she gives me a friendly smile. "Good job on your dance."

Is she *serious*? "Thanks!" I blurt as she passes, her spine straight and graceful.

At last! I rush into the bathroom, grab my backpack, and pull out my cell phone. There are *five* texts from Amelia.

The first makes my heart stop:

running late, sorry!

ok we r leaving!

in the car!

aunt h drives 2 slow!

c u SOON!!!

I need some details here. *How* soon? *Because I need to be back in my clothes and at Weehawken Middle School by four o'clock. Not to mention I don't know one step of your dance from Act Two, and the star of the Bolshoi Ballet wants my head on a plate.*

I text back:

where r u??? help!!!!!!

As I wait and wait for her answer, my heart starts to pound like a kettledrum. Tell me she's not out of cell range!

She must be, because there's no answer.

What should I do? I'm dying to wash off this stupid doll makeup and put my own clothes back on and flee for school. That's what I *want* to do. But I promised I'd wait till Amelia gets back. What if she gets held up in traffic and misses her Act Two duet?

Exactly. What if? Do I want to go out onstage and swan-fake *that* in front of an audience? There's no way!

I guess I could pretend I was injured. Or sick, that'll work. I've been coughing and sneezing, pretending to be nauseous. . . . A sudden attack of Black Death plague? That should keep them away from me.

I'm going crazy. Where *is* she? The intermission must have started by now. This can't get any worse.

Someone pounds on the door.

It's Lara, I think. *Or her sister. Lara* and *her sister!*

I'm not going to open that door. They can't make me.

"Diana, it's me!"

Thank God! Amelia!

I throw open the door and she rushes into the bathroom, red-faced and still wearing her soccer uniform. "I am *so* sorry!" she gasps. "How'd it go?"

"Long story," I say, so relieved I'm afraid that I'm going to start crying.

Amelia nods, pulling her jersey off over her head. "Let me get into that dress."

I unzip it and peel off my tights. "These are kind of gross."

"What, and I'm not?" says Amelia, pulling off her cleats and shin guards. "I smell like a sweat sock."

The bathroom is not all that big, and we keep bumping into each other as we change clothes. Next comes the makeup. I cover my fingers with cold cream and swipe at my face with a towel as Amelia opens the jar of clown white.

We're both standing in front of the mirror, and it's like a time-lapse photo: one doll face off and one doll face on.

"How did the tryouts go?" I ask Amelia as she frantically slathers clown white on her forehead.

"I aced it. We both got accepted."

I slap her five, then think of something. "But what will you say to your mom? She must know when the tryouts were held, and that you couldn't be there."

Amelia shrugs, drawing pink circles on both of her cheeks. "I'll tell her they made an exception for me. Because I'm so exceptional."

Hmm. I guess I'm not the only person who stretches the truth to her parents sometimes. But there's one more thing I have to tell her. "Amelia? I, um . . . sort of messed up. Big-time. Diva Central is ready to kill me. Kill *you*."

"What did we do?" asks Amelia, penciling on her fake eyebrows.

I wince. "Kicked a ballet slipper at her. And then dropped your soccer team jacket on top of her head. Off a sandbag."

"For real?" Amelia stares at me, one eyebrow white and one black.

"I'm so, so, so sorry," I tell her. And she bursts out laughing.

"No sweat. She deserves it!"

That may be true, but Diva Central is *furious*. She's out for blood. There's a sudden sharp knock on the door. We look at each other.

"It's *her*!" I whisper, my eyes bugging out. "Nikolai must have told her where you get dressed!"

The knock comes again, this time with a boy's piping voice. "Amelia? It's Eli. It's time for our dance!"

Whew.

"Right out!" calls Amelia. She dots on her lipstick and whispers to me, "You're gonna be great in *The Snow Queen*."

She leaves, and I look at myself in the mirror. I sure hope she's right, because right now I feel like the world's biggest flop.

I sprint all the way to the school and arrive just a few minutes late for the four o'clock speed-through. It's not a disaster, since I've only got the one cue for my solo, but it's *unprofessional*, something that I hate to be. Plus I'm out of breath and completely convinced I'm a walking disaster, about to strike twice.

I come skidding into the back of the auditorium, running past Will in his sound booth. The work lights are on, and the whole cast is standing onstage in a loose circle, shaking their hands out as Ms. Wyant leads a group warm-up.

Gracie Chen's sitting in the front row with her clipboard. "Sorry," I hiss as she checks off my name, sternly telling me, "Six minutes late!"

I rush up the side steps to the stage and join the group circle, shaking my arms, then my shoulders, and then flopping down from the waist.

"Like a rag doll," Ms. Wyant instructs us.

Funny, that's just how I feel.

Usually it would calm me down to be back with my friends, going through our familiar preshow routine, but today I'm too rattled to go with the flow. As we're bouncing in place, exhaling huh-huh-huh-huh sounds, Jess catches my eye from the opposite side of the circle. She shoots me a questioning look, then flashes me a thumbs-up, then a thumbs-down. Which one is it?

I don't even know how to answer. All thumbs.

When the warm-up is finished, Ms. Wyant says, "Excellent! Thank you, young stars!" Then we start on the speed-through. These are always goofy, with actors in street clothes rattling through their lines triple-time. I don't *have* any lines, just my song toward the end of Act One, so maybe I'll finally get to relax. If I can.

Kayleigh asks, "Are we going to run songs?"

Oh, god, that's all I need. If I miss that high note now, there's no way I'll get through it tonight.

Ms. Wyant says, "No, I want you all to save your singing voices. Just lines, and sound and lighting cues."

Thank goodness! So I really do have some downtime. For the first time I realize I'm not only exhausted but *starving.* I never ate lunch. I can't wait to dig into one of those subs!

"Tell me all," whispers Jess as we settle into two seats in the auditorium. "Did Amelia get back in time?"

"Barely."

"How was your dance?"

"I stunk," I tell her. "And I nearly killed Diva Central."

"You're kidding me. How?"

I tell Jess the whole story in hushed tones. When I get to the part about the soccer jacket falling out of the sky, she's laughing so hard that Ms. Wyant turns around and says, "Sssh!"

"Sorry!" I mouth. Jess and I sit side by side, trying to stifle our giggles. As soon as one of us pulls it together, the other one loses it. Our shoulders are shaking. Tears run down our cheeks. It feels so good to laugh like this.

Suddenly Jess sobers up in a hurry. "Oops," she whispers, "I'm in the next scene. Check you later."

There's nothing that tastes quite as good as a giant sub sandwich when you're really hungry. It might be the sheer size that makes it so delicious — the roll is as long as two desks — or the mix of cold cuts, cheese, sliced ripe tomatoes, and lettuce, but this is the best sandwich I've ever eaten.

All over the music room, actors are scarfing down sandwiches, too. I notice that Riley is standing with Marisol, and Ethan and Jess are together, their heads leaning toward each other. Hmm. Ethan . . . and *Jess*? I never would have guessed that from the way they make fun of each other. Maybe I'm imagining things.

"Great sandwich," a boy's voice says over my shoulder. I turn, and it's Will. My stomach does a little flip-flop. "So what was so funny?"

"When?" I ask.

"During the speed-through. I was in back at the sound booth, and you and Jess were, like, *shaking*."

"Oh, right," I say. "I almost murdered a mean ballerina."

"Cool," says Will. He's looking at me with an odd, intent stare, and I suddenly feel super self-conscious. "Diana, I think . . ." he starts.

Is Will going to say something *boyfriendy*? Right here and now?

"I think you've got some mayo right . . . *there*," he says, rubbing my eyebrow. "That's funny. It doesn't come off."

"It's probably greasepaint," I tell him, hyperaware that his finger is touching my face. Even if he's just trying to rub off a smear. "You know, from Amelia's doll costume?"

"How did it go?" Will asks.

"Remind me never to dance ballet," I say. "Actually, you won't have to remind me. I *know*."

"I bet you did fine," says Will. He's stopped rubbing my eyebrow but still seems to be staring at me in that weird way. "I brought you a present," he mumbles.

I'm astonished. "Like for opening night?" Is that my heart making that noise?

Will shuffles his feet, dipping his head so his bangs fall in front of his eyes. "Opening night, or for Christmas, or . . . here." He shoves a small shopping bag at me. Inside is something wrapped up in white tissue paper. "It's not really wrapped."

"Oh," I say, blushing as I remember my impulse buy. "I've got a present for you, too. It's not really wrapped either." I unzip my backpack and take out the tissue-wrapped T-shirt I got him at Kim's Golden Treasures.

"Let's open them at the same time," says Will. "One . . . two . . . three . . . go!" I reach into the bag as Will unwraps his T-shirt.

"You're kidding me!" he exclaims as I pull off the tissue, revealing —

The very same T-shirt!

Well, not exactly. Mine has a geisha on the front instead of a samurai, and the electric guitar she's holding is hot pink, not red.

"Did you get this at Kim's Golden Treasures?" I ask, and Will nods, grinning.

"It reminded me of your pink guitar in the Tasha Kane video."

"Yours reminded me of you playing the bass," I say.

We look at each other, happy and breathless. And then Will leans forward to give me a hug. "Thanks," he says into my ear, and as he pulls back, I feel his lips graze my cheek.

Was that . . . a *kiss*?

It's almost seven, and Gracie has already given a ten-minute call. We're all in full costume, checking our makeup and fluttering nervously. Jess flaps the arms of her clown suit. Riley watches as Marisol reapplies lipstick. Kayleigh strides back and forth, doing weird vocal warm-ups, as if to let all of us know she's a Serious Actress.

"Diva alert," smirks Ethan, but I shake my head. I know what a *real* diva is now, and Kayleigh is not even close.

I take a deep breath, or try to. I've got the worst case of opening-night jitters *ever.* My confidence is totally shot after messing up in *The Nutcracker*, and I'm shaky from Will's sort-of kiss. I feel like a soda bottle that got opened too fast, spilling bubbles all over. The intercom's on, and above all the greenroom noise, we can hear the adrenaline-pumping sound of a large, eager audience gathering.

"It's a full house!" says Ms. Wyant, coming backstage with her trademark wide smile. "All right, young stars, circle up."

We gather into a circle, and she looks around at our faces. "You've all done incredible work during these last days and weeks. This is the part where each one of you digs down way deep and shows everyone what you're made of. Energy *up*! Voices *up*! I want to see a *spectacular* show!"

She extends her hand into midcircle, and everyone piles their hands on top like the Three — or the thirty-three —

Musketeers. "And, GO!" says Ms. Wyant. We lift up our hands with a roar so loud that the audience must hear it right through the wall.

True to the cliché, last night's horrible dress rehearsal has somehow transformed into a wonderful opening night. As I stand in the wings, I gaze out over the darkened audience. There are familiar faces everywhere: I spot Mrs. Munson and Dash; Sara, sitting with her aunt Himani; Gracie Chen's grandparents. I grin extra wide when I spot Nelson Martinez, dressed to the nines as always, sitting with someone who must be his *date*!

Front and center, of course, sits my very own family. Fay is on one side, actually smiling for once, and Ashley and Brynna look . . . excited. Impressed, even. To be seeing *me*. How funny. Dad is in the aisle seat, looking totally proud.

I glance all the way to the back of the house, where I see Will's face over the sound console, and feel my heart beat even faster.

This is the second time in one day that I'm waiting in the wings to go onstage. But there's one really big difference, I realize. Instead of being in somebody else's costume, about to go out and fake something I really don't know how to do, I'm in my element, surrounded by people I love.

The scene I've been watching comes to an end, and the audience claps as the curtain swirls shut for the snow scene transition.

This is it. Time to go out there and cast a spell.

I take a deep breath, holding on to my magic staff and feeling the comforting weight of that beautiful cloak on my shoulders. Miss Bowman starts playing the familiar chords of my solo. As I make my entrance, the light catching the points of my icicle crown, I hear somebody gasp. I bet Nelson is beaming.

Behind me, the stage crew bustles around, quickly transforming the palace gardens to chilly white winter. All the things that were worrying me fall away as I start to sing.

The song unspools like a dream. Finally, I lift up my magic staff, gathering all my spirit and energy into that last soaring high note. As I raise up both arms and feel the glorious music flying out of my mouth, I'm filled to the brim with joy.

Yes! I stand in the spotlight in front of my family, my friends, and — now I can finally say it — my *boy-friend*, Will.

This is my world, I think happily. This is exactly where I belong.

Take a sneak peek at

Petal Pushers

An irresistible new series about four sisters and one hectic flower store . . .

I stepped forward and opened the door. "Welcome to Flowers on Fairfield," I said in my most professional-sounding voice. "Can I help you?"

The woman looked to be in her midtwenties. Her long, blonde hair was pulled into a perfect ponytail, not a strand out of place. She had big, blue eyes and was wearing light pink lipstick. She was just so pretty and perfect looking, like a mannequin.

Oddly enough, she had her hands in the air, as if she was afraid to touch anything. *Maybe she's one of those germphobic weirdos,* I thought.

"I just got a mani-pedi!" she exclaimed as she stepped inside. "Don't want to smudge my nails!" She smiled, flashing her straight, white teeth. I found myself nodding in sympathy and returning her grin, although I wasn't totally sure what she was talking about. Manny who?

"Oh, okay," I said.

"Would you be a sweetheart and put Louis on the floor?" she asked me.

"Louis?" I asked.

She looked at me like I had two heads. "Louis Vuitton?" she said, nodding toward the bag slung over her shoulder.

That's when I noticed that there was a tiny, shivering dog poking its face out of her large purse. I reached inside and picked up the dog. As I placed the pet on the floor, I blinked. Was Louis wearing a tiny, black leather motorcycle jacket? Why, yes he was.

The customer looked around. "So this is it," she said with a sigh. "I was hoping it would be . . . fancier."

My mouth fell open. How rude! Luckily, Gran sensed my annoyance and stepped right in, putting on her most gracious smile. "How can we help you, dear?" she said.

"My name is Olivia Post," the woman said. She held out her left hand. A huge diamond sparkled on her ring finger. "I got engaged last night!" she gushed. "Five carats, cushion cut, can you believe it?"

We all oohed and ahhed although I don't know if any of us knew exactly what "cushion cut" meant. "So," Olivia continued. "I wanted to have a spring wedding. May nineteenth!"

Gran smiled, but she looked distracted. I knew she was calculating how many weeks that would give us. Her widened eyes said it all — not many.

"Will it be a large wedding?" Gramps wanted to know.

"Oh, only a couple hundred guests," explained Olivia.

Gramps and I exchanged glances. That was huge by anyone's standards!

"But I really want it to have an intimate feel," Olivia continued. "And it's got to be special. I'm thinking ice sculptures, a couple of chocolate fountains, a sushi station. . . . So the flowers, of course, have to be exquisite," she concluded.

Gran looked panicked. In two weeks she and Gramps were going to be snorkeling with the sea turtles. *Would* my mom be able to handle this? Slowly, Gran shook her head. "I don't know if this is a good time," she said. "You see, there's going to be a change in management. . . ."

I cleared my throat. "There's no problem at all," I heard myself saying. *Wait! Stop!* my brain protested. But my mouth kept moving. "We will give you the wedding of your dreams. The most exquisite floral arrangements this town has ever seen!"

Everyone stared at me in shock. Except Olivia. She just smiled at me as if twelve-year-olds routinely took charge of planning weddings. “Excellent!” she said. Checking her nails, she picked up Louis Vuitton. Then she whipped out her cell phone and placed a call.

“Hello. I am interested in ordering six dozen white doves, spray painted pink,” she said on her way out.

The door shut behind her. “Oh, Del, you were great!” cried Gran, giving me a squeeze. Then she looked into my eyes. “Do you really think you can handle it?”

“No problem, Gran,” I said. My heart was pounding. I could hardly believe it. I had just agreed to do the flowers for an impossible-to-please Bridezilla with unrealistic expectations. In a matter of weeks, no less.

My stomach sank. What had I gotten myself into?

Life, Starring Me!

Callie for President

Drama Queen

I've Got a Secret

Confessions of a Bitter Secret Santa

Super Sweet 13

The Boy Next Door

The Sister Switch

Snowfall Surprise

Rumor Has It

The Sweetheart Deal

The Accidental Cheerleader

The Babysitting Wars

Star-Crossed

Accidentally Fabulous

Accidentally Famous

Accidentally Fooled

Accidentally Friends

How to Be a Girly Girl in Just Ten Days

Ice Dreams

Juicy Gossip

Making Waves

Miss Popularity

Miss Popularity Goes Camping

Miss Popularity and the Best Friend Disaster

Totally Crushed

Wish You Were Here, Liza

See You Soon, Samantha

Miss You, Mina

Winner Takes All